CAPTAIN COMBAT:
THE SKY BEAST OF BERLIN

THE SKY BEAST
OF BERLIN

By Barry Barton

STEEGER BOOKS • 2021

CHAPTER 1
SATAN'S HEADQUARTERS

O F THE some four and one half million persons who resided within the limits of greater Berlin on August 25th last year, not over half a dozen had ever been inside the large steel-walled room located in the basement of the grey stone building across the street from the German Chancellery. As a matter of fact it is doubtful if more than a score of persons in all Germany knew of its existence. That steel walled room was the heart, the nerve center and the spider's nest of the Third Reich. It was the spring that fed the Nazi cesspool of death and destruction.

On this twenty-fifth day of August, four high ranking Nazis were seated about one of the tables in the room. One was Hermann Peiplow, chief of the *Nachreichtenamt*, the Intelligence Corps of the Third Reich. Another was Franz Khole, head of the Gestapo, the ruthless, and often stupid, Secret Police. A third was Doctor Wolfgang, chief of the Department of Scientific Warfare. And the fourth was Karl Lundz, director of Sabotage Operations. A description of each is unnecessary. One has only to know that they looked exactly what they were… four of Satan's henchmen.

The object of their meeting was a letter Hermann Peiplow had placed on the desk before him. It was postmarked Posen,

Poland, and was addressed to Mrs. Charles B. Combat, Imperial Hotel, Berlin. The letter read:

The Heinkel burst into flames and started for its watery grave.

CAPTAIN COMBAT

My dear Sister:

I am stopping here at the Europa Hotel for a day or so before going on to London. Why don't you and Bill join me and we will return home together? In view of unsettled conditions, believe it best for you two to cut short your vacation trip. Not that I wish to appear an alarmist, my dear. Still, I think it would be best for us to remain in England until the present mess blows over. Wire me the time of your arrival, and I will meet you at the air field.

Affectionately, your brother,

Harry.

Peiplow tapped the letter with a stubby finger and stared at Franz Khole, of the Gestapo.

"A very innocent letter, perhaps," Peiplow murmured. "What do you think? You have treated it for invisible writing, of course?"

"Of course," Khole nodded. Then, referring to a little note book he took from his pocket, he began talking as though he were a schoolboy reporting to the teacher on his subject of research for the night before. "Mrs. Combat is the sister of Lord Harry Brainbridge, attached to the British Foreign Office. In 1917 she married an American World War ace, named Charles Bates Combat. Combat was killed at the Front in November, 1918. The son, William Combat, was born on Armistice Day at the American Hospital in Paris. He was educated in the United States and England. He served two years in the Royal Air Force, and is a captain in the R.A.F. reserve. For the last six months he and his mother have been touring Europe on a sort of vacation. The object of the trip, however, was to permit young Combat to study aviation on the Continent. Of course, he is appearing as a civilian observer, being connected with the Hawker-Vickers Co. It is assumed, however, that he will make a complete report to the British Air Ministry when he returns home."

The Gestapo chief paused a moment and waited for permission to continue. Peiplow gave him that permission with an abrupt nod.

"We believe that both the mother and son are acting as unofficial agents of the British Intelligence," Khole continued. "And that this letter is no more than an order from Lord Brainbridge to report to him and get out of the country before it is too late. Agents, of course, are watching Brainbridge closely in Posen, but they have reported nothing of importance, as yet. I suggest that the letter not be delivered and that the Combat woman and her son be detained. I believe things should be arranged so that—they disappear, eh?"

The Gestapo chief accompanied the last with the closing of one beady eye, and a faint crooked smile. Peiplow did not reply.

He sat frowning down at the letter and absently drumming his thick fingers on the table top. After a moment he raised his head and stared about the room. A dark flush of pride filled his face, for this room was the dream of his life, ever since the day *Der Fuehrer* had elevated him to a position of supreme power. Within those four walls dwelled the means of contacting any point in the entire world by phone, radio, or television. Shelves held volumes of intricate naval, military, and aviation codes; teletype machines brought him instant information from land, sea, or air. Other shelves held files; complete data on everybody of importance who was either a friend or an enemy of the Third

Reich. In fact, so well equipped was the room that by the mere flick of a switch Hermann Peiplow could—by radio wave, the secret German *Blau* wave—explode a mine fathoms down in the English Channel, or in the Mediterranean, or in Hong Kong Harbor—or even in New York's Hudson. In short, Hermann Peiplow could fight a war for Germany, destroy forts, bomb cities, sink ships far at sea, and not once step out of that steel-walled room.

YES, THAT room was his diabolical pride and joy and he could sit for hours gazing at the instruments of doom—within easy reach of his thick, stubby fingers. Presently, though, he turned his gaze to those gathered about the table.

"Perhaps a worthwhile suggestion, Herr Khole," he said slowly. "But to destroy them might raise complications. Their disappearance might cause Brainbridge to suspect we are aware of him. That we wish to avoid for the moment. For the present, the Leader wishes it to appear we are friends of the British; that wish no war with them. When the Leader marches into Poland—then all will be different. Besides, that young fool, Combat, cannot have learned much of importance. He has not the intelligence—"

Peiplow suddenly stopped and fixed cold eyes on Doctor Wolfgang's pasty face. The head of Scientific Warfare had suddenly started slightly, and was biting his lower lip.

"You have something to say, *Herr* Doctor?" he demanded.

"For one thing, I agree with *Herr* Khole's suggestion," the Doctor said. "As you know, some of my papers regarding the Blau wave were stolen last month. Their loss is not great. But the English are not all fools. If those papers should reach their hands…"

The Doctor paused for a moment and scowled. "I would not be pleased if that happens," he said presently. "Then too, there is the matter of our ships in New York. The Bremen. We know that the Americans are going to delay her. We shall then have to use our magnet planes. No, I do not think it best for us to permit either Brainbridge—or the Combat mother and son—to return to England. No, not even though the mother and son are American citizens. What do we care for public opinion in the United States? They are all blind cattle in America. No, in case they *are* reporting to Brainbridge, I think it best…"

The Doctor left the rest unsaid, but the gesture he made with his hands was plain to all. The other three at the table nodded—although Hermann Peiplow still frowned slightly.

"I will talk with *Der Fuehrer* first," he said. "What the Leader orders shall be done. Meantime, this letter will be delivered and we will do the usual routine work, of course. That, *Herr* Khole, I leave in your hands. You, *Herr* Lundz, had better return to Posen at once. And you, Doctor, back to your laboratory. *Der Tag* approaches on fleet wings. Germany is ready and eager to prove its might once and for all. For twenty-one years we have waited. No power on earth can stop us now. Civilization must be taught its lesson."

With a nod and a wave of his hand, the Intelligence Chief dismissed the others from the room. When they had left he stood straddle-legged, hands on hips and arms akimbo, gazing about the room. His eyes glittered, and his face muscles twitched with savage emotion, for Hermann Peiplow could hardly wait for the order from the Leader to start spilling blood over a jittery and nerve-frayed world.

CHAPTER 2
MYSTERY IN BERLIN

THE BROAD-SHOULDERED, six foot youth with the handsome, sun-bronzed face caught the instant attention of every *Fraulein* in the lobby of the Imperial Hotel as he came swinging in through the street door. He also caught the attention of the clerk in back of the desk. The clerk hissed a few words to the switchboard operator and that young man instantly shoved a contact plug into its place. As that was being done, the clerk hurried out from behind the desk and intercepted the tall youth on the way to the elevator.

"You are looking for your mother, *Herr* Combat?" the clerk asked politely. "I believe I saw her go out into the gardens. Shall I send a page?"

Bill Combat flicked a cigarette butt into a sand jar and shook his head.

"Not in her room?" he grunted. "No, never mind the bell hop. I'll go look for her myself. Any mail for us?"

"I will look at once, *Herr* Combat," the clerk said. "Would you care to come over to the desk?"

Combat followed him over and waited while the clerk fussed around the mail slots. It took him two or three minutes but he was unable to produce anything.

"No, there is no mail, *Herr* Combat," he smiled. "You were hoping for a letter, *ja?*"

"Who doesn't, when he's away from home?" Combat grinned, and swung away toward the gardens at the rear of the hotel.

He walked among the flowers and met several ladies who would have been only too glad to chat with him. But he did not see his mother, so he kept on going. Finally, when he had made a tour of the grounds, he went back into the lobby. And he entered it just in time to see his mother doing the same thing from the street side. He hurried over to her and kissed her on the cheek.

"Been shopping, Mom?" he asked and led her toward the elevators. "Just got in myself. No soap again. They wouldn't let me within a mile of the Heinkel plane factory. As if I hadn't flown their new bomber a half dozen times. Do I know what a spy must feel like, now! Darn it, Heinkel has a welding torch that would save us a lot of money at Vickers. It's the one thing I came here to see."

He would have gone right on talking if his mother had not stopped him with a quick glance as they stepped into the elevator. Bill Combat was like that. Once he got started on matters pertaining to aviation and all its ramifications, he was good for hours in front of any listening audience. But no one ever interrupted nor grew bored, because when Combat talked on aviation he was worth listening to. However, as he caught her quick look he shut up, and in silence they rode up to their suite.

As they walked down the hall they passed two men who automatically bowed. Combat hardly gave them a glance, but when he and his mother entered the little sitting room of their suite he suddenly stopped and stood motionless in the middle of the room. For some reason he had a sudden premonition that all was not as it should be. The feeling was gone in a moment, however. And it was then that he saw the worried look on his mother's beautiful face.

"What's the matter, Mom?" he asked. "Anything happened?"

Mrs. Combat peeled off her gloves, removed her hat and sank down in a chair. She looked at her son, and drew a slender hand across her forehead before she spoke.

"I think we should return to England by the next plane, Bill," she said. "I don't like it here. The tension in the air. There's something brewing, and we're much too far from home. I… I feel as though hidden eyes were watching us every second. Let's go home, shall we?"

"Why sure, Mom, sure, if Berlin gets you!" he cried and dropped to one knee by her chair. "But every foreigner is watched in Berlin, if that's what you mean. You should have been with me this morning at the Heinkel plant. I'll swear they had a machine gun hidden behind a screen in the production manager's office. And did I get the bum's rush! Confound it, when are the heads of nations going to stop snarling at each other so that the rest of the world can sleep at night?"

His mother said in a low voice: "Speaking of this morning, shortly after you left, a dressmaker shop called me up. I'd never heard of them. They begged me to come see their new designs. The woman on the phone had tears in her voice. I had to agree or hang up on her. I went down and they didn't have a model less than a year old. And they didn't seem at all interested in my buying anything. It's strange. I mean…"

SHE STOPPED and frowned in perplexity. Bill Combat started to grin, to laugh away her crazy fears, but somehow neither the grin nor the laugh materialized. His keen, steel-trap brain was clicking back over the last half hour. The desk clerk had never shown him such courtesy before. And the man had taken a long time to find nothing in the mail slots. Now, a crazy phone call to his mother. Those two strangers who had bowed in the hall. And that funny feeling he'd had when he entered the suite.

He stood up and began slowly surveying the room. When his gaze rested on the top of the desk in the corner, he stiffened, and then stepped quickly over to it. On one corner of the desk was a pile of papers—data on foreign commercial aviation that he had collected during his tour. They would form his report to the Vickers company. There was nothing secret in any of the stuff, for anybody could obtain it.

However, the papers were not in the exact neat pile in which he had left them, and there were two or three other things on the desk not exactly as he'd left them. The desk was his workshop, more or less, and his mother never went near it. And the maid had strict orders not to tamper with it, dust or no dust. To make sure, he turned and asked his mother if she had touched anything.

"You know I wouldn't, Bill," she replied quietly. "Why? Is there something missing?"

He shook his head silently, then motioning to her not to

question him further for the moment; he began an inspection of the entire suite. When he returned to the sitting room his brows were furrowed and his eyes steely bright.

"Somebody is worried about us," he said aloud, more to himself than to his mother. "And from what I've read of Nazi cleverness, they certainly must have assigned a dumb ox to this job. Son-of-a-gun! Those two that passed us in the hall, of course!"

"What are you talking about, Bill?" his mother asked in a nervous voice.

He laughed and went over and put his arm around her.

"Steady, sweetheart," he chuckled. "Nothing to worry about at all. Those Gestapo lads can't keep their long noses out of anything, you know. Our suite has been searched."

"Then…?" his mother gasped and stopped, one beautiful hand to her throat.

"The reason for that dizzy phone call," he nodded and gave her another hug. "Crude wasn't it? What did the fatheads expect to find, I wonder? I believe we burned those secret plans of my design of a plane that flies backwards to keep the dust from the pilot's eyes didn't we? And that vest pocket disappearing howitzer you and I whipped up one morning before breakfast?"

"Please, Bill," she said in a voice that shook a little. "You're not funny. I'm worried. Why should our suite be searched? Why?"

"Routine precaution, probably," he said, but somehow his words didn't even convince himself. "I think I'll ask the management, though. After all, we're traveling on American passports, and…"

The rest was interrupted by a knock on the door. Combat opened it. The bellhop outside held a letter in his hand.

"This just arrived in the post, *Herr* Combat," the bellhop said. "The clerk thought you might be expecting it."

Combat tipped the boy and took the letter. He saw that it had been posted in Posen, Poland, and he instantly recognized his Uncle Harry's hand on the envelope. A frown creased his brows for a moment, then he suddenly squinted hard at the sealed flap, took it over to the window for a better look. Presently he gave it to his mother. "To you from Uncle Harry in Posen," he said. "And I rather suspect that it has been opened." His mother took it without a word and tore open the envelope. They both read it together.

My dear Sister:

I am stopping here at the Europa Hotel for a day or so before going on to London. Why don't you and Bill join me and we will return home together? In view of unsettled conditions I believe it best for you two to cut short your vacation trip. Not that I wish to appear an alarmist, my dear. Still I think it would be best for us to remain in England until the present mess blows over. Wire me the time of your arrival, and I will meet you at the air field.

Affectionately, your brother

Harry

P.S. Arrange to arrive here on the evening plane on Wednesday, the twenty-seventh.

NEITHER OF them spoke for a moment after they had read the letter. Kidding and joshing would fall flat now. Certainly there was a war just around the corner, now, else Uncle Harry wouldn't have suggested their return to England. His letter meant that all hope for peace was gone; that Hitler was going to march. Uncle Harry was in a position to know, and he was telling them so in his short note.

"I get it, now," young Combat grunted. "No wonder the place was searched. You and I are spies for England, Mom, did you know that?"

"Bill, what in the world do you mean?" she gasped.

He snapped the letter with his index finger. "Uncle Harry's job at the Foreign Office," he said. "They undoubtedly know here in Berlin that he's connected with Intelligence, too. The Germans simply did some quick, and cockeyed adding and figured we must be a couple of Uncle Harry's agents. Don't forget, I've been wading around knee deep in aviation over here. So it's war? The madmen!"

His mother nodded silently and stood looking at him. Her memory went back over the years to that day she had met the good-looking American Air Service officer at the English Overseas Club dance in Paris; back to the day when she had married that Yank pilot; back to the days when she had moved to Paris to work as a Red Cross nurse so as to be near him; back to those long weeks of waiting for her child to be born, and to that day the news had been told to her…that Charles had been shot down in flames. She remembered vividly the day Bill was born, and all the suffering, the heartache, the soul-chilling misery. And now…another war! One had taken the only man she ever loved. Would this new one take Bill, her only son?

14

"We'll go back to England, Bill!" she said suddenly and fiercely. "Then back to New York. Your father made us Americans, Bill. War here in Europe is none of our business. Come, we'll start packing at once. Ring for the maid, Bill."

Herr Wolfgang

"Here! Whoa—and stop worrying!" the son cried and grabbed at her as she hurried across the room to the closet where the bags were. "Uncle Harry said Wednesday, the twenty-seventh. That's not until tomorrow. We can't sit on packed bags for twenty-four hours. We…"

Young Combat stopped short as his gaze came to rest again on the letter on the table, where his mother had tossed it. For some reason that amazed and confused him the letter seemed to hold a new and entirely different attraction. He read it through again, and when he got down to the postscript he suddenly realized what was wrong. Whatever the Germans might know about Lord Brainbridge, there was one thing about the titled

15

Englishmen of which they were obviously in the dark. That was his almost fanatical passion for neatness and orderliness.

"So Uncle Harry didn't write that P.S.," Bill Combat whispered to himself. "That throws the border margins all out of line. Uncle Harry would write a letter all over again rather than send out one like this."

He picked up the letter and stared hard, at the postscript, but he was not enough of an expert to detect any proof of forgery. Nor did he have testing equipment with him. Yet, deep inside of him he knew that Lord Brainbridge had never written that postscript. Who had? Somebody who wanted his mother and him to remain in Berlin until plane time on the twenty-seventh. Why? What difference did it make? He had not the slightest idea, but a tiny bell of warning was sounding within him, and the back of his neck began to crawl as it had often done during his life when unpleasantness was ahead of him. Unpleasantness and danger.

He slipped the letter into his pocket and crossed the room to where his mother had remained motionless, watching him intently.

"We can pack later, Mom," he said. "How about going out now and find a new place for lunch, huh? I'm hungry as a bear."

"We can have something sent up," she suggested. "Why do you want to go out? It looks as if it's going to rain."

"Maybe these walls have ears," he said in a low voice. "A restaurant won't. Besides, you and I are going into a huddle, Mom."

She started to ask him why, then shrugged and went for her

hat and gloves when he gave a quick shake of his head. He was her son, and so she could tell that he had suddenly become more than a little worried himself.

CHAPTER 3
INVISIBLE DEATH

B ILL COMBAT'S mother toyed with her cup of tea and gazed thoughtfully around the tiny restaurant where they were just finishing a late lunch. Eventually she brought her eyes back to rest on his good-looking face, and tried to smile slightly, in spite of her inner doubts.

"You make it sound like a movie scenario, Bill," she said. "And although what's happened has upset me, I can't help but feel that your plan really will get us into trouble. What earthly reason could they have for wanting us to stay here another twenty-four hours? Jumpy as I am, I must say it all seems a bit too ridiculous."

"It probably is," he said slowly and mashed out his cigarette. "And frankly, I certainly hope so. I hope I'm all wet about Uncle Harry not writing that postscript. But—well, with things popping so fast these days, I guess I would feel better if we were both out of Germany."

"But to sneak out of the hotel, Bill, as you suggest!" his mother exclaimed. "That *would* look funny. Why not go to Posen a day earlier and wait for Uncle Harry? Simply check out of the hotel."

"And be stopped!" Combat said. "And if that wasn't Uncle Harry's postscript we *will* be stopped. Why, and what for, I can only guess. I... I'm playing a hunch, Mom. If the laugh is on

17

me, then it's okay. But I don't think there'll be any laugh. So we do it, Mom?"

His mother was silent a long moment before she nodded.

"Yes," she murmured and shivered a little. "Perhaps it would be best."

"Swell," he grinned and his blood began to tingle with the excitement. "Now, we'll have dinner at the hotel and go up to our suite as though for the night. I'll even leave a call with the desk clerk. In our suite we'll shove a few things into the over-night case and then slip out and down the stairs that lead into the gardens. We'll go separately and meet at the street gate. It will look as though we were going for a stroll. That overnight case of yours is no bigger than a purse anyway. And we won't have been seen by the desk clerk. Once on the street we'll take a cab to Tempelhof Airport in time to catch the night plane to Paris. Our passports are in order, so that's that. Once we're in Paris we can send for our luggage. Okay, Mom, let's get out of here and get some air."

Sometime later, Combat and his mother rode up in the Imperial Hotel elevator to the floor of their suite. The youth had already left a morning call at the desk, and as the car rose he was trying to picture the clerk's face in his mind. Had there been a funny look in the clerk's eyes? Hadn't just the ghost of a smile flitted across the thin lips? Combat wasn't sure, but more than ever he was convinced that flight from Berlin that night was a very sane idea.

Once they were in their suite, his mother turned to him and stared intently up into his face.

Captain Combat

"You still think we should, Bill?" she asked. "After all, we *are* American citizens, and… Well, I don't like the idea of running away from anyone."

"And I like it less, Mom," he said softly. "But the old hunch keeps telling me not to take chances. Maybe we'll laugh at this

19

tomorrow. But right now, go toss what you want into your bag. This aviation stuff I can stick in my pockets."

Some twenty-five minutes later Mrs. Combat looking rather guilty, and not a little worried, blew a kiss to her son and went out into the hall. Young Combat grinned after her, closed the door and started walking around the room to kill the ten minutes before he would slip down to meet her at the garden gate.

"I'd like to see the look on that clerk's face when he learns we jumped the hotel bill," he chuckled. "Gosh, but Mom is swell. But I've got to get her out of Germany. It doesn't look so good at all."

He walked over to a vase of flowers on the table and absently inspected them. Inspected them, yet wasn't conscious of doing so because his thoughts were elsewhere. They were back in England; in the British Air Ministry to be exact. If Hitler marched into Poland, England would be honor bound to stand by her agreement with the Poles. That meant England would declare war on Germany. He was on the Royal Air Force reserved list. He had served two years with the R.A.F. simply to add to his general aeronautical education. But if England declared war, he would have to report to the Air Ministry for duty. He'd…

HIS THOUGHTS suddenly became oddly hazy in his brain. He turned from the table to go into the bathroom for a drink of water, but stumbled to his knees by the time he'd taken two steps. At any other time he would have forced himself up on his feet, gasped with puzzled annoyance and tried again. But this time he didn't. He clamped his lips shut, grabbed his nose with thumb and forefinger and locked the air in his lungs. Then, crouching low, he waddled like a duck to where his coat and hat lay on a chair, and from there over to the door.

A splitting pain cut across his forehead, and it seemed ages before he could grasp the knob of the door and twist it. Once outside in the hallway he pulled the door closed, straightened up slowly and leaned one shoulder against the wall. Spear points of flame were darting all through his body, and everything in the hallway seemed completely out of focus. The almost overwhelming desire to sit down and close his eyes came to him. Heart pounding furiously, he fought back the urge for blissful sleep and forced himself to move slowly along the hallway.

When he had gone a dozen steps or so he released the clamped air in his lungs, and then refilled them. The effort left him strangely weak, but only for a moment. The sharp pains abated considerably and objects held steady in his vision. He swallowed hard once or twice, took one steely-eyed glance back at the suite door, and then walked rapidly to the stairs that lead down to the gardens.

His mother was waiting there just outside the gate, and he greeted her with a grin. A grin that he had to force to his lips, for there was no doubt about anything, now. By the narrowest of margins he had escaped death. Perhaps it had been those flowers. He didn't know. Perhaps the odorless gas had come from something else in the room. He had no way of telling. But he knew beyond all doubt that sinister minds had arranged for Mrs. Charles B. Combat, and her son, William, to die in Berlin's Imperial Hotel. And he also was equally positive that the news-paper-reading world would have been informed that it had been suicide. A suicide by common gas stove fumes, no doubt.

The truth infuriated him as much as it mystified him. However, he made no mention of it to her as they walked along the street toward a taxi stand a few blocks down. Tomorrow, perhaps he would tell her. But what she didn't know now would worry her less. The rats! The dirty, stinking rats. But why did anyone want them to die? The only reason he could think of was because of what he'd said to his mother in a more or less kidding way—that the Nazis believed them to be secret agents operating for Lord Brainbridge, of the British Foreign office. Why they…?

He cut short the rest as the street suddenly resounded to the eerie wail of a fire engine siren. And a few seconds later one of the Berlin pieces of fire apparatus roared by. It was the emergency truck, complete with pullmotor, oxygen tanks, and so forth. And when it braked to a stop at the curb in from of the Imperial, Combat gritted his teeth. The rats had even timed the whole thing. They had even arranged for the emergency truck to come rushing up. It couldn't be otherwise, because if a maid or anybody else, such as that thin-faced desk clerk, had entered the suite, they wouldn't have found either his mother or him. But they were making it look perfect, because they were quite confident they would find two dead people in the rooms, and were therefore acting accordingly.

Unconsciously quickening his pace Combat hurried his mother down the street and handed her into a cab. As the cabby turned his head for directions, Combat pursued his lips in thought, and then turned to his mother, who sat patiently beside him.

"Tempelhof is quite a sight at night, Mother," he said, speaking in perfect German. "Would you like to drive out and watch one or two of the big transports land?"

"Yes, I think that would be nice," his mother replied, but he saw that the knuckles of her hands clutching her bag were white. Gamely, but obviously, she was concealing her feelings.

"All right," he said cheerily. "Tempelhof, driver!"

CHAPTER 4
MIDNIGHT MADNESS

A S THOUGH the gods were on their side for the moment, the floodlights were turning Tempelhof Airport into high noon as they drove up. In the distance a huge Hansa transport was gliding down, its wide silver-tipped wings causing it to look like some prehistoric bird returning from another world. Hastily paying off the driver, Combat led his mother into the waiting room, and through it and out onto the wide veranda that flanked the embarking ramp. It was an hour before the Paris plane was due to leave, so there was plenty of time in which to get tickets and have their passports checked. But, as a matter of fact, he wanted to delay getting the tickets as long as possible. The effects of that strange gas that had almost clipped off his life were still with him, and for the time being he was content to just rest there and gulp in the cool, refreshing night air. Also, it always did give him a thrill to watch the big sky babies come swinging down onto the landing runway.

And so they watched the activity about the field for a half an hour or more, until the public address system announced the departure time of the Paris plane. The voice sent a chilling note to Combat's heart, but he immediately cursed himself for a jittery fool, and led his mother into the little coffee and sandwich shop just off the veranda.

"Order a cup for me, Mom," he said, "while I go get our tickets."

She smiled and nodded, but her face was pale and her beautiful eyes were tinged with fear. She hadn't spoken more than a half a dozen words since their arrival at the airport. It struck him as though she had retreated within herself and was battling something she could not put into words. And with his thoughts concentrated on his mother, he almost collided with a man in uniform brushing past him toward the ticket window.

Sight of the uniform, rather than the near collision with its wearer, brought Combat up short. It was one of Hitler's pet Storm Troopers, and he shoved people aside as if he were wading through a herd of sheep. At the ticket window he stopped, glared importantly at the man behind the grillwork, and snapped his fat lips apart.

"Show me the passenger lists for all outgoing planes!" he barked.

"There is only this one, the Paris plane," the ticket seller replied meekly and handed a sheet of paper to the Storm Trooper.

That very important stuffed pig ran his eye down the list and scowled with disappointment.

"It's two Americans I seek!" he grated and flung the list back. "A woman and a man, her son. You checked the passports?"

"But, of course!" the ticket seller assured him. "And none was a woman."

The Storm Trooper snorted, turned and flung an arrogant look about the waiting room, as though daring anybody to challenge his authority, then stalked out to the passenger embarkation platform. There he would wait and personally examine every passenger and passport that went aboard the plane.

However, several seconds before Hitler's hired thug had ceased his conversation with the ticket seller, Bill Combat had turned in his tracks and was hurrying back into the coffee shop. His mother, looking up, saw his face and the look in his eyes, and started to speak. A barely perceptible shake of his head stopped her words. A waitress was placing coffee and buns on the table.

"We can't stop for this," he said and placed some money on the table. "I phoned Franz and he said for us to join him by all means. He'll have food and drink there, of course. Come along, my dear."

With an apologetic smile for the waitress he took his mother outside by a side door, and down onto a promenade that led along one side of the field, where there were hangars for private and visiting planes. As soon as they were out of earshot, his mother could restrain her curiosity no longer.

"What now, Bill?" she demanded. "You looked as if you'd seen a ghost back there in the coffee shop."

"Not a ghost, a Storm Trooper," he said quietly. "The lad was asking for an American woman and her son. He…"

"Bill!"

"Steady, Mom," he soothed. "Yes, they sure don't want us to leave. All the airports and rail stations are being watched, obviously. They certainly found out darn quick."

"But how could they?" his mother gasped. "I don't understand. I… I feel very strange, Bill. I so wish this night were over. What are we going to do, Bill? Shouldn't we better return to the hotel and try to find out what it's all about?"

FOR A split second he was tempted to tell just why the Imperial Hotel would be the last place they'd go to, but he killed the thought. They were two people—marked for death by the Nazis. For what reason, he could only make a wild guess. However, he most certainly wasn't going to bother finding out. He and his mother were going to leave Germany…tonight!

"Going back might only lead to trouble," he said gently. "We're caught in some kind of a crazy net, Mom, and our best bet is to get out of it as fast as we can."

"But how?" his mother moaned in desperation. "What can we do but go back? Oh, you mean hide in some other hotel? But, our passports, Bill! You always have to show your passport when you register at a hotel."

He didn't answer for a moment. He stared down the promenade at the assortment of planes lined up in front of the hangars. They ranged from sport single seaters up to five passenger cabin jobs. And as he stared, a reckless plan took form in his brain. Reckless, yes, but it was their only chance. Storm Troopers and members of the Gestapo were probably combing Berlin for them now, and the longer they remained the slimmer their chances were. For a moment he hesitated, and then memory of the Imperial Hotel decided him definitely.

"We're going to play being two crooks again, Mom," he said with a chuckle, trying to take some of the fear from her eyes. "First we jumped a fat hotel bill, and now we're going to commit a theft. Well, let's say we're going to borrow some German flying enthusiast's plane."

"Bill, you're mad! We—couldn't possibly!"

"It will be a cinch, Mom," he corrected her and pointed. "Look down there. At least a dozen ships with their props ticking over. The private fliers go in for night flying a lot over here, but they have to stick close to the field. We won't. See that neat little low wing, two-place open cockpit monoplane down at the very end? Not a soul near it. The owner's probably gone for coffee. That's our aerial taxi for tonight. It's fast, and she'll get us over the border with gas to spare. If there's an emergency tank on that particular make of ship, we should even be able to reach Paris."

"I say you're still mad, Bill!" his mother protested.

He took a firm grip on her arm and walked her forward toward the far end of the plane line. "Never more serious in my whole life, Mom," he said evenly. "Please don't argue. Believe me, we've got to leave Germany tonight…or perhaps we never shall."

She looked sideways at him, made as though to speak, but thought better of it. She shivered a little, made a queer little sound deep in her throat and then increased the pace. He grinned when really he wanted to stop and take her in his arms and hug her. Objections, yes, but no slobbering and womanish wailing about it. He was proud of her courage. IT TOOK them two minutes to get

close to the small but fast plane, and then—it took another five to make sure nobody was paying any particular attention, for the owner appeared to be nowhere in sight. Then he led her around to the other side, where there were shadows, and helped her to hoist herself into the front pit. A second after she was settled, he was in the rear pit, releasing the wheel brakes and reaching for the throttle in one continuous motion.

The inverted water-cooled engine in the nose roared up with its song of power. The tiny ship trembled and quivered and then virtually leaped forward like a race horse leaving the barrier. Instinct, more than anything else, caused Combat to twist his head around as the plane rocketed out across the airport's surface. As he did he saw a helmeted figure come racing along the hangar apron. The man's mouth was open and he was obviously shouting, though of course Combat could not hear a sound above the engine's thunder. The running man was waving his hands wildly.

Hardily conscious that he was doing so, Combat raised a hand in salute, then lifted the plane clear of the ground and went curving up and around toward the night sky. The flood lights had been turned off, but there was plenty of light about the Paris plane at the loading ramp. Combat glanced down at it and imagined that one of the figures moving about was the blustery Storm Trooper.

Turning front, he reached forward over the cowling space that separated the two pits and patted his mother on the shoulder. She turned her head, got it into the prop-wash and instantly made a wild grab for her hat... and lost. It went sailing out and away, and the prop-wash promptly tried to take her lovely rich chestnut hair along with it. She laughed as she ducked down behind the windshield and brushed the hair from her eyes. Combat laughed, too, with relief, and wanted to start singing a song. That he had come close to dying that night was practically forgotten history, now. They were on their way to Paris while Storm Troopers combed Berlin. Score one against the Nazi butchers. They might be hot shots when it came to dealing with their own breed. But a couple of Americans...

A brilliant shaft of light cut through the night like a knife, and the rest of Combat's thought died in his brain. He jerked his head around and immediately stared into a sea of dazzling white as the swinging searchlight beam found his plane and held it like a tiny moth impaled on a long thin spear.

CHAPTER 5
FUGITIVES' FLIGHT

FOR PERHAPS a full second, Combat stared down that shaft of dazzling white light. And then suddenly there came a sound akin to the bark of a Saint Bernard, and off to his right a red and yellow ball of fire burst into being. His heart skipped several beats and the blood ran cold in his veins. The damn Nazis were signaling him by anti-aircraft fire to return to the field immediately. He didn't have to guess twice. That fat Storm Trooper, realizing that a plane was being stolen, had put two and two together, probably for the first time in his life, and had ordered the searchlights and the signal shell.

"Bill! Are they shooting at us?"

His mother's voice came to him as little more than a whisper above the roar of the engine. He didn't bother to tell her by hand or motion. The searchlight beam still stuck to him like glue, and he knew that unless he shook it off the next archie shell would come much too close for comfort.

"Hang on, Mom!" he bellowed.

Even as the words burst from his lips he slammed the joystick over and stepped hard on the right rudder pedal. The fleet little plane slashed over and down in a neat half roll without so much as a tremor rippling through its frame. Out of brilliant light into equally blinding darkness Combat plunged. He waited two fearful seconds, then pulled the ship up out of its dive onto level keel and went veering off to his right.

By then his eyes had become accustomed to the darkness. He

didn't have to glance at the altimeter. A look down over the side told him that he was about two hundred feet off the ground, and a glance backward showed that he was at least a good mile from Tempelhof Field. But that glance backward told him something else—something that caught his breath in his throat and made his two hands gripping the stick go clammy with sweat. Two Nazi interceptor planes were taking off.

Twisting front, he snapped off the wing lights and even the dash cowl light, then banked more toward the east and jammed the throttle forward to the last notch. Holding his hand against it, as though in doing so he might get extra speed out of the ship, he and his mother went rocketing through the black night.

Not too sure of the terrain that stretched out ahead, he wasted forward speed for a bit until he had climbed to seven thousand feet. There he ran into cold air and the windshield was of little help. The cold cut through his light clothing like a knife, and he clenched his teeth to stop them from chattering. He realized that his mother up in the front pit was suffering equally if not more so, and he was sorely tempted to slide down into warmer air. But he refused to do so for the very plain reason that he did not dare. He would rather risk the cold than the possibility of slamming headlong into a hillside.

And so he held his altitude and went roaring forward. Every so often he sighted a cluster of lights on the ground below him and he guessed from his compass direction that they were the towns of Seelow, Lebus, Kustrin, and Drossin. If that were true, and there was no reason to believe that it wasn't, they were on a crow's flight course for the Polish border and Posen, some sixty or seventy miles beyond.

Suddenly, as he picked up the lights he believed to be the German town of Blesen, the night sky became laced with searchlight beams. By the act of God, not a single one of the shafts of light caught his ship in its white glare. But he knew it would be but the matter of seconds before that came to pass. And to stave it off as long as possible, he decided to risk low altitude and slide earthward. A moment later the sky above him became dotted with anti-aircraft bursts and his heart turned to ice in his chest. Those archie burst were no precautionary measures, simply because the sound of his engine had been picked up. He didn't even have to guess to know that word of his escape had unquestionably been flashed to the entire German border—along with orders to shoot on sight. The Blesen batteries had heard him, naturally, and so were attempting to do that very thing.

However, it was not the idea of archie fire that chilled his blood. It was the realization that the archie fire was more or less a signal. Behind him in the black sky somewhere, Nazi planes were hunting for him. The two he'd seen take off from Tempelhof had been the new Heinkel type, and he knew, of course, that they were fitted with two-way radio. In a split second, Blesen could inform the searchers aloft that he was approaching the town, and every plane hunting for him would converge on Blesen from the four points of the compass.

"Hedge hop around it to the south," he muttered aloud, and hunched himself forward over the stick. "It's my only chance. Ten to one they won't look for us low down."

Trusting to his eyes, and the relation of the plane to the lights of Blesen off to his left, he slid down until blurred treetops were but fifty feet or so beneath the belly of the plane. There he leveled off and began skirting the south of Blesen, his nerves drawn taut like violin strings. He released one hand from the stick long enough to reach forward and tap his mother on the shoulder.

"Okay, Mom?" he yelled. Then he added, "Some fun, huh?"

The face that was turned toward him was little more than a faint blur, but he fancied he saw the flash of white teeth in a smile. Then came her voice faintly. "I know you'll beat them, Bill dear!"

The meaning in the words sent tingling warmth rippling through him. A fellow just couldn't lose with a mother like that in the cheering section. The bursting archie shells and the deathly seriousness of the situation was undoubtedly clutching at her heart, just as it was clutching at his. But did she complain? Did she go haywire with fright, like a million other women might? Not a chance. Not *his* mother!

THEN PRESENTLY the lights of Blesen were far behind, and the archie shells no longer dotted the black heavens with their gobs of yellow-red. And ahead of him was the Polish border and safety. Another half hour and he could look back into Germany and thumb his nose in joyous derision.

Only a half hour more at the most!

But a bare fifteen minutes of that time had clicked off into history when the gods of good fortune turned their backs on that small plane racing eastward over Germany. Down out of the black sky whirled a bullet-spitting winged chariot of death.

And even as the first ship came gun-yammering down, a second one off to the right took up the chattering chorus.

The instant the sounds of machine gun fire crackled against Combat's ears, he stepped on right rudder pedal with every ounce of his strength and slewed the small ship around in a crazy flat turn. No sooner had the plane responded to his movement of the controls than he changed over and sent the ship cutting back in the opposite direction. Back and forth he zigzagged as death poured down from above. Not once did he bother to look up. It would be impossible to tell the type of planes in the darkness, and as a matter of fact the type didn't matter a damn.

A savage fervent prayer on his lips, he belted the fleet little plane all over the sky, ever nearer and nearer to the Polish border. True, his attackers had speed to burn, but he had a hunch that maneuverability odds were in his favor, and so he recklessly pushed his advantage to the limit. So long as he made himself a poor target he had a chance. But that wouldn't last forever. Searchlight beams had sprung into action on the ground and the shafts of white light were starting to bracket the entire heavens.

The urge to shout comforting words to his mother swept through him, but when he opened his lips he discovered that his throat was dry from excitement and tension. So he gave up the idea and continued to hurl the ship relentlessly about the sky. As he came out of a flash half roll, he suddenly spotted a fountain of ground signal flares ahead, and knew instantly that they came from Polish border patrols leaping to the alert. Not three miles away. Perhaps not even two.

"We'll make it, Mom! We'll make it!" he screamed in a voice that sounded like somebody tearing a piece of tin.

As the words rushed off his lips, he ducked away from the blur of flame-spitting black lightning that was slicing down from the right, and the instant he was in the clear he shoved his own nose earthward and went diving toward the flares on the Polish side of the border. In the next split second the entire German side of the border fountained bursting archie shells up at him. He even believed he heard the chatter of ground machine guns, but that might have been simply the echo of the guns on the two Nazis planes above him.

Suddenly, when the border was directly beneath his wings, the engine in the nose sputtered loudly. The sputtering changed into a sharp metallic splintering, and almost immediately the engine sounded as though the pistons were tearing and ripping their way through the cylinder walls. Instinctively he realized that a burst of bullets from one or both of the Nazis planes had crimped and twisted his metal propeller, and that it was furiously vibrating itself into slivers of steel, with its tip clipping the leading edge of the wing for good measure.

Instinct and action became one. He shot out his hand, hauled back the throttle and snapped off the ignition in one movement. Then his hand flew to the landing gear lever and he lowered the wheels. He was over Poland now. The Nazis planes had turned back at the border, but he did not believe the pilots had done so out of respect for international boundary lines. In fact, he knew exactly why as he took a quick glance upward into the search-light-laced sky. Polish planes were hurtling forward toward the border—a half-dozen of them—and no Nazi pilot would stomach a three-to-one fight.

LAUGHING AND sobbing with joy, Combat guided the little crippled plane down toward a flat section of ground he could see in the glow from the searchlights. And in another half minute or so the ship was on the ground and he was gingerly wheel-braking it to a stop. The moment it came to a halt he stood up in the cockpit, climbed out of it, and moved forward on the wing stub until he was beside his mother. With a wild cry of joy he flung both arms about her.

"We did it, Mom!" he cried. "This is Poland. We're safe, now. We're…!"

He stopped with a gagging sound, and bent his head close to her. The fingers of his left hand had suddenly become wet and sticky. His heart thumped against his ribs and stopped. He put his other hand under her chin and lifted her face.

"Mother!" he cried. "Mother!"

Her eyes fluttered slowly open, and a sound like a faint happy sigh slipped off her lips. "I knew you'd get us here, dear," she whispered. "Good boy, Bill."

He hardly heard her voice, for in the faint light that still hung in the heavens, he stared frozen-eyed at the glistening crimson stain that spread from her shoulder up across the base of her neck.

"God, Mom!" he choked. "Steady, Mom, dearest, I'll get a doctor. There must be one near here. We'll get you to a hospital."

"It doesn't hurt, Bill, dear," she whispered in a fading voice.

"Really, it doesn't. Just don't leave me, Bill. A doctor wouldn't help. You were wonderful, Bill. I'm proud of you."

"Proud of me?" he cried in heartbroken anguish. "Of *me?* I did this to you, Mom! I forced you to come, and…"

"No, dear," she said softly. "It was the only thing we could do. It wasn't your fault, Bill. It… it just had to happen, I suppose. And… and it doesn't hurt. I just feel… a little sleepy, I think. Bill, dear, Bill?"

"Yes, Mom?" he said brokenly.

"Take care of yourself, Bill, won't you? I suppose you'll be going to war, now. Remember, Bill, your… your father and I will forever be watching over you. Watching over you, and… and proud that… you're our… boy. Goodbye… my… darling."

"Mom!"

His hoarse cry echoed across the lonely field, but she did not answer. Her eyes were closed. Her beautiful face was calm and placid in the pale light, and there was even the ghost of a smile on her lips. It was as though a bare second before her heart stopped beating, she had had a glimpse of the peace and ever-lasting happiness that was ahead. It was as though the fighting eagle who had died in flames twenty-one years ago was reaching down to her from God's Kingdom.

For a long minute Combat stared down into her face as bitter misery and remorse tied his heart and soul into knots. He did not even see the Polish officer and a party of border guards approaching. He was conscious only of his mother's face... her face, even more beautiful in death than it had been in life. Then, as a choking sob shook his whole body, he put both arms about her again and held her pressed close to his breast. He raised tear-filled eyes toward the heavens and prayed in a hoarse, choking voice.

"Let me live, dear God in Heaven! Let me live until I have wiped every last one of the stinking devils from the face of the earth. Dear God, I beg only that. Only that!"

As the last left his lips, the hot bitter tears coursed down his cheeks, and he bent his head and buried his face in his mother's rich chestnut hair.

CHAPTER 6
SATAN'S ORDERS

HERMANN PEIPLOW sat frowning—at his desk in the steel-walled room that served as the nerve center for Nazi hate and ruthlessness throughout the Third German Reich. For several moments he had been sitting there, his lips curled in a snarl and his gleaming black eyes fixed on the wall.

Suddenly he smashed the desk with his clenched fist, snorted with impatience, and went over to a panel on the wall that was covered with knobs and switches. There was a set of headphones on a hook, and built into the center of the wall was a small mike. By flipping a switch, Peiplow could instantly make contact with any given point on the globe. The switch he flipped up now, however, simply took him to Tempelhof Airport, a few miles away.

"Sir?" came the polite voice in the earphones as he whipped them over his head. "Number Twenty-Six reporting."

"Reporting what, you dog?" Peiplow roared. "Where are those planes? They should be back by now. I contacted them myself. I'll give them but ten minutes to get here to my office. Relay that to them at once, you understand?"

"Yes, *Herr* Peiplow," the voice at the other end said. "I will do as... Just a minute, sir! Planes are coming in to land, now. Yes, it is *Oberleutnants* Meuller and Blye. An airport car has gone out to meet them."

Peiplow grunted and slapped down the switch. Then, with a flick of his hand, he twisted one of the many knobs and flicked up another switch. Almost instantly a voice said, "Forty-nine reporting, sir," it said. "I have news."

"Then don't waste time!" Peiplow grunted. "What is it?"

"One of my men was able to get close to the American's plane, sir," the man at the other end spoke. "He has just this minute made his report to me. It was not a crash landing as I first stated, sir. The American, *Herr* Combat, was not injured though his mother died. I shall have my man follow him, sir?"

As the agent in Poland reported to his superior, Peiplow's

veins stood out at his temples and the gleam of death itself blazed in his eyes.

"Follow him?" he bellowed. "You dundering *schweinehund!* You and your fool will come back into Germany at once. You are through. You get close to the American and then just walk away? *Mein Gott…*"

"But it was impossible to use a gun, *Herr* Peiplow!" came the whining voice over the wire. "A party of Polish troops and an officer were with him, and…"

"Silence, swine!" Peiplow roared. "A few pig Poles, eh? And your man runs like a rabbit? Report to me personally, both of you. I'll show you what you should have done. I'll…"

The sound of a pistol shot coming over the earphones stopped the Chief of Nazi Intelligence. For a split second, wonder lighted up his eyes. He called into the mike, but when there was no reply he grimaced and took off the earphones.

"The dog had sense enough to put a bullet through his brain," he growled and walked back to his desk. "He knew that I would do it for him when he arrived. *Mein Gott* I will kill them all, the *dummköpfs*, if they let that American slip through their fingers. He must die as his mother did. *Der Fuehrer* has so ordered. And it shall be done, even if I have to do it myself!"

The man dropped into his chair and crashed his fist against the desk again and fell to staring and frowning off into space once more. A little more than ten minutes later, a green light on his desk winked rapidly. He straightened up, slipped a hand under the edge of the desk and pressed a button. Then he twisted around in his chair and glared at the steel door as it swung slowly open.

IN THE small hall outside stood two men, neither of whom was more than twenty-five years of age. They wore the uniform of the Nazi Air Force, and the rank of *Oberleutnant* was on their shoulder straps. Stiff as a pair of fence posts, they saluted the Chief of Nazi Intelligence. Peiplow grunted in a half sneer, motioned them into the room, and then pressed a button that closed the door behind them. For a moment or so he kept switching his gaze from one to the other, and then finally let it come to rest on the taller of the two.

"Well, Meuller," he said in a voice that sounded like gears clashing, "perhaps you expect me to decorate you with the Iron Cross, First Class, eh?"

The red rushed into the pilot's face. He licked his lips nervously. "The American was in the air before we received orders, *Herr* Peiplow," he began. "We did not know what direction he would take. And so…"

"You fool!" Peiplow thundered. "Would an escaping man fly deeper into a trap? *Mein Gott,* where else would he try to fly but to the nearest frontier?"

"Yes sir," the pilot said meekly. "We decided that, too. So we gave chase. But he flew without lights, and it was not for some time that he was heard from the ground and his position radioed to us. When we did reach him he was very close to the border."

"And I beg to state he was in a fast plane, *Herr* Peiplow," the other pilot spoke up. "Also, that he was no fool at maneuvering."

"Of course he was no fool!" Hermann Peiplow grated. "He

was a clever swine. No wonder that dog Brainbridge used him as one of his agents. But you two seem to miss the point, I think."

"The point, sir?" one of them murmured politely.

"Yes, the point!" Peiplow snapped. Then, as his eyes became like two black ice cubes, "The *Fuehrer* issued orders that the dog of an American and his mother were not to be allowed to leave Germany alive. At the hotel there was failure to carry out the Leader's orders. At the airport there was also failure. You two failed in the air. And two more of my men stationed in Poland also failed. Counting you two, that makes a total of eleven who failed the Leader, and failed me. Eleven German lives for two swine American lives… and one of the Americans still lives!"

The German's words rang about the room, hit the steel walls and echoed back and forth until an electrified silence stilled the sounds forever. Wide-eyed, the two pilots stared at Peiplow. And then suddenly the true meaning of what had been said burst through into their brains. They both stiffened, then Meuller spoke in a hoarse frightened voice.

"It is not fair, *Herr* Peiplow!" he cried. "It is not an easy task to find one small plane in the black sky at night. We did our best. I swear to you that we did our best. *Herr* Peiplow, you cannot…."

"I cannot?" the Nazi blood letter boomed and leaped to his feet. "You had your chance, and you failed—both of you. Failure will not make Germany the greatest nation upon this earth. Our Leader has never failed. I have never failed. We accept nothing but success. And blundering fools like you are of no use to the Third Reich!"

His black eyes boring them, Peiplow reached out and jabbed

a button. As though by magic a door opened in back of him and a bull-necked staff major entered the room. Peiplow didn't even turn his head. He kept his eyes fixed on the two white-faced pilots.

"Take care of these two traitors," he barked. "Have the Bureau of Public Information publish their names, and the time of execution. It will serve as a warning to all others that to fail Germany is to die!"

As though a spell had been cast upon the two doomed pilots, they walked mechanically from the room, eyes fixed ahead and not glancing to the right or left. When the door had closed upon the pair and the bull-necked major, Peiplow walked once more over to the knob-and-switch-studded panel on the wall. Eyes glittering and his jaw muscles bunched, he angrily snapped up switch after switch. Then, when a whole row of lights was on, he bent his head toward the microphone.

"Official orders to all agents!" he barked. "Drop all assign-ments and search for an American somewhere east of Posen. Name, William Combat. Height, about six feet. Steel blue eyes, brown hair. Wearing civilian clothes. Probably heading for Posen to meet Lord Brainbridge of British Intelligence. The Leader orders Combat to be killed at all costs. Kill him even if you have to kill Brainbridge, too. It is too late to be careful, now. Combat is a menace to the Third Reich. Kill him, and report to me at once. Failure will cost you your lives. Start at once!" Peiplow had spoken to the men with authority, and now that his voice had stopped, he seemed to speak with his eyes the grim determina-tion that he felt.

CHAPTER 7
AGENT SIXTEEN

LORD BRAINBRIDGE'S hand trembled as he poured some whiskey into the glass. His usually ruddy face was drawn and white and he studiously avoided Bill Combat's eyes as he handed him the drink.

"No, I'll blame myself to my dying day, William," he said with an effort. "I'm responsible for my own sister's death. Your mother, my boy. I should have used my head. Should have realized that the dirty Nazis would believe you two my agents. That was the answer, of course. They hate me, just as much as I hate them. God… I can still hardly believe it's true. I feel so terribly for you, my boy. Your mother was a wonderful woman. She…."

The big man stopped talking, groaned and rubbed a hand through his iron-grey hair. Bill Combat said nothing. He stared unseeing down at the drink his uncle had given him. Two days had passed since that horrible night. Two days? Maybe two years, or two centuries—he didn't know. And all that had taken place since was one great jumbled picture of events, most of which his tired brain could hardly remember. Once he had made known his identity to the Poles, unlimited sympathy, courtesy, and understanding had been given him. They had helped him bury his mother, right there in the field where she had died. He might have been able to take the coffin back to England, but with invasion and war practically hours away, it might have been impossible. And somehow the feeling had come to him that she would have wanted to be laid to rest at that spot. At any rate, there she had been buried under the guns of a Polish guard of honor.

After that, there had been the journey back through the Polish lines of trenches and defense works to Posen. He had been in Posen a whole day and night before he'd met his uncle, for duty had called the Intelligence man away. Eventually they had met at Brainbridge's hotel, and a few moments ago, Combat had finished telling his story. He clamped down on his nerves, took a long drink, and then forced his uncle to meet his eyes.

"Your fault—or mine—it doesn't matter, now," he said in a dull voice. "She's gone, and perhaps it's the way God wanted it. England will declare war?"

"No doubt about it," Brainbridge said. "Even Chamberlain admits that, now. When Hitler marches into Poland we declare war on him. And he's going to march! Nothing in Heaven or in hell will stop that madman from attacking Poland."

"Then I'm going to England by the next transport plane!" young Combat said in a hard voice. "I'm going back into the R.A.F. America can stay neutral, but by God I'm going to fight. They took my father long ago, and the lousy Nazis took my mother. I'm going to help wipe them from the earth if it's the last thing I do. Are you coming with me, Uncle Harry? Is your work here done?"

The other didn't answer for a moment. He stood sipping his drink and staring out the window, across the housetops of Posen, then turned and looked at Combat.

"No, not yet, William," he said in a low voice. "In a way, my work here has only begun. I..." Brainbridge seemed to stumble over his words. He paused a moment, swallowed and cleared his throat. "Perhaps you can serve England best by remaining here in Poland with me, William," he finally said.

"How?" Combat asked, and he was vaguely surprised at the lack of interest in his voice.

If Lord Brainbridge noticed it, he at least gave no sign. He simply motioned to Combat to finish his drink.

"We'll take a little walk, William," he said putting down his glass. "In these damnable times it's safe to talk only in the open air. Nazi agents and Gestapo men practically live in hotel room walls."

"Yeah," Combat grunted and stood up. "Like cockroaches."

When they left the hotel, Brainbridge led the way across the city to a park. There he found a bench that had neither a tree nor a shrub within fifty yards of it and sat down, motioning Combat to join him. The Englishman calmly and deliberately took out his pipe, crushed shredded tobacco into the bowl, and got it smoking before he said a word.

"It's really a long story, William," he began, "but time's precious, so I'll give you the highlights. They should give you an idea of what we're up against. Well, regardless of all the soft soap Chamberlain swallowed at Munich, the Foreign Office and Intelligence were not lulled to sleep by Hitler's words. We knew war was coming, and so did every Englishman with half a brain. Well, when war *did* come, what would be our real problems?"

"U-boats and aircraft," Combat said before the other could go on.

"Exactly," Brainbridge nodded. "Because of the Maginot Line,

46

the Belgian Line, and so forth, land fighting wouldn't be a problem. At least, not right at the beginning, anyway. No, U-boats, aircraft, plus any and all secret weapons the Nazis would spring on us. U-boats we

learned how to handle in the last war. The convoy system, I mean. And bottling them up in German ports. Aircraft we'd have to handle with our own planes, anti-aircraft guns, and so forth. Well, to double check, we sent agents swarming all over Germany. Double the number already stationed there. Orders were to send back anything they uncovered, no matter how unimportant. Well, two very important things came to light, and on both subjects we know hardly anything."

BRAINBRIDGE PAUSED a moment and savagely sucked on his pipe. It had gone out, but he seemed not to realize that. The look in his pale eyes was distant and far away....

"And in a way that's why your mother was killed," he suddenly said softly. "God, what a fool I was not to have seen into the future, not to have realized the possible great danger to you two—traveling all over the Continent. And in Germany, of all places!"

"Better explain what you mean," Combat said in a tight voice.

The other gave him a guilty side glance and grunted.

"Sorry, William," he mumbled into his pipe stem. "Well, one of my best agents got wind of two German secrets. He was able to steal some papers that contained enough information to make us pretty sure that the Germans had developed a new kind of radio wave. They can explode mines at great distances, we believe. How, we don't know. We simply know that it can be done. The other item is that a British navy blockade against U-boats would be utterly useless. The U-boats will be able to come and go out of German ports just as though our warships weren't there waiting outside the Baltic."

"How?" Combat asked when the other stopped abruptly.

"I don't know," was the blunt answer. "The agent who reported both things to me died in my arms. He was shot from a passing car as we walked down a street in Warsaw. Just like your American gangster pictures. He had been followed, of course, though he was so sure of himself. But he died with whatever else he could tell me locked in his brain. He gave me the papers he'd stolen, but they were practically useless. He'd stolen them from the laboratory of a Doctor Wolfgang, head of Nazi Scientific Warfare. He'd just given me the bare outline of what he'd discovered, and then the bullets from that passing car hit him. As he died, though, he whispered one name—Heinrich Staube. He begged me to see Staube, and then took his last breath on this earth."

Brainbridge stopped talking again, and stared out across the park. His jaw muscles bunched and deep lines came to the corners of his eyes. Combat waited grimly for him to continue. The words came after a moment or so.

"A name whispered by a dying man on the sidewalk of a Warsaw street," Brainbridge said viciously. "Obviously a German, but where would I find him? I had no idea. That was a month ago. Since then I have done little else but try to find a man named Heinrich Staube. I contacted every agent I had in Germany. I hunted high and low... and yesterday I found out. Staube is a ship's carpenter living in a town called Pinneberg, near Hamburg. He is too old for naval service. His wife was a Jewess, and she died in a concentration camp. There are no children. He is broken in health and the townspeople consider him a little mad. Of course, no one man gave me that information. Sometimes one of your own men turns out to be a damn Nazi spy. Once I had located the man, I took measures of finding out about him. But he is the one my agent begged me to see."

The older man fell silent again, went through the motions of relighting his pipe, and then suddenly turned so that he faced Combat.

"I shall probably never be sure, William," he said heavily, "but I believe it was because of my agent that your mother was killed. You and he looked something alike. My letters to you two caused the Gestapo to wonder. They checked, probably, and somebody took you for my real agent. They included your mother, naturally. They knew papers had been stolen and they became alarmed. To have murdered you with Germany still at peace with England would have looked bad, so they tried to make it appear as suicide, or accidental death. Failing, they really became alarmed and— God curse them, the yellow dogs!"

Combat clenched his fists, dug his teeth into his lower lip and said nothing. Both sat silent and brooding for three or four moments. Then Brainbridge broke the spell.

"IT IS impossible for me to go see this man Staube, William," he said. "I would be recognized the instant I stepped onto German soil. Even here in Posen the Nazis watch every step I take. The place is overrun with them. Poor Poland! She'll be stabbed in the back as well as shot in the face when Hitler marches. Anyway, I wouldn't be able to get near Staube. And at the moment there is no agent within call whom I would trust with the mission. True, it may prove nothing. Yet, it was that agent's dying plea… his dying advice to me. William, you might serve England more than either of us can imagine right now, by going to Pinneburg and finding this man Staube. My agent would not have used his last bit of strength to beg me to see the man were it not of vital importance."

"I think you're right about that, Uncle Harry," Combat said. Then, with a shrug, "I'll do anything to hamstring those Nazi rats, but I wonder how good I'd be as an Intelligence man. I…."

"Never mind the modesty!" Brainbridge said almost gruffly. "If ever a man had Intelligence work training, you have. You speak several languages perfectly; you know how to conduct yourself according to the situation confronted; you are an expert pilot; you've received special technical training; you're a fighter; you've got courage, guts. And you've got a damn good head on you. There's Brainbridge blood in you, William. Dammit, what...?"

"All right, Uncle Harry!" Combat said, and smiled for the first time in three days. "Maybe all that I lacked was confidence, and you've given it to me. Of course I'll go. What are your instructions?"

Brainbridge smiled and reached a hand over and patted him on the knee. "Good lad, William," he said, and meant it. "Modesty is such silly rot, you know. When a man's good, dammit, he should admit it. My instructions? Carry your life in your hands, my boy, and trust no one. Get to Pinneberg and find this Staube. He may know my agent by number. It was Sixteen. Perhaps Staube was in Sixteen's pay. We Intelligence lads often hire civilians for small jobs, you know, and pay them from our own pockets. In that case you'd better know the word that will identify you to any member of British Intelligence. It's Mons."

"Mons," Combat repeatedly softly. "The first battle of the last World War!"

"Part of England's history," Brainbridge said grimly. "Now, tonight I'll take you to a place here in Posen where you'll be fitted with a German passport and anything you need—such as cash and that sort of thing. At midnight you'll board the Hamburg plane, and...."

Lord Harry Brainbridge, of the British Foreign Office, attached to British Intelligence, stopped talking right then and there. At least, Bill Combat didn't hear him say anything else. Instead, he heard a sharp *twang* off to his left, and almost instantly a ribbon of white flame zipped across the base of his neck. As though a fist had crashed against his neck from behind, he pitched headlong off the bench and down on hands and knees onto the gravel path.

Another *twang* came to him, but he was unable to place its direction. Unable to, because cannons were booming in his brain and bells were clanging in his ears. Instinctively he tried to push himself up onto his feet, but he seemed paralyzed from the waist down. His legs were like poles of rubber attached to his hips. From a long ways off he could hear his own voice cursing at his useless legs, but they simply gave way under the weight of the rest of his body, and he sprawled on his face.

In an abstract sort of way he knew that he had been shot at and hit. Hardly realizing it, he fumbled in his jacket pocket for the small Luger that a Polish officer had given him. But he couldn't pull the damn thing out. It was stuck in the pocket lining and refused to be budged. He heard running feet close by and fear made sweat ooze out on his forehead and trickle down off the tip of his nose. In one desperate effort he tried to lift his head, to force himself up. It was impossible. It was as though the weight of the world itself was on his shoulders and Bill Combat was buried forever.

And then there came to him the stifled moan of a man in deep pain, and an instant later a heavy body crashed down on top of him. He was knocked flat, his straining arms collapsing under him. And before he could make another move, he went swirling away on the turbulent waves of a roaring black ocean from which there was no escape. He fought against the million sensations that seized him.

CHAPTER 8
DAWN OF DOOM

WHEN BILL Combat next opened his eyes it was to find himself in a hospital cot. His head was full of dull throbbing. Gradually, though, objects took definite shape. He saw that a nurse sat by his bed. The little insignia on the lapels of her white blouse told him she was a member of the Polish Medical Corps. At the foot of the bed stood a pleasant-faced officer of the Polish military police. And beside him was another Pole, evidently, though he wore civilian garb.

All three of them stared quietly at Combat, and he simply stared back at each of them in turn. The Polish military police officer smiled and broke the silence. "You are feeling better, Mr. Combat?" he asked in perfect English.

"I'll get by, I guess," Combat murmured. Then, as memory did not return in very clear detail, he asked, "Just how did I get here, and where is Lord Brainbridge?"

The three looked at each other and sort of bowed their heads a little.

"Lord Brainbridge is dead," the military police officer said softly. "He was dead when we reached the spot of the attack. You were still alive, so you were rushed here by ambulance. You saw who shot you, eh?"

Combat simply shook his head. He couldn't speak. First his mother, and now Uncle Harry! God in Heaven, was he a death jinx or something? The Nazis had trailed him to Posen, found him and tried to kill him, believing he was reporting to

Brainbridge. Memory of the white pain at the base of his neck returned, and he understood how his uncle had died. The killer had shot wide. The bullet had creased the back of his neck, evidently nicked a nerve that caused the paralysis, and passed on to smack straight into Uncle Harry.

"Was Lord Brainbridge shot just once?" he asked with an effort. "In the face?"

"That is so," the police office replied. "Two shots must have been fired. The back of the bench was split by one bullet. The one that killed Lord Brainbridge was from the new German Mauser rifle. Pardon, Mr. Combat, but you were a friend of Lord Brainbridge, yes?"

"He was my uncle," Combat told him. "Perhaps you read in the papers what happened two days ago at the frontier west of Posen? That was his sister the German rats killed. My mother. I was flying the plane."

As Combat spoke, the atmosphere in the room underwent a sudden change. A tension, which even he had begun to feel, suddenly disappeared. The curious and cautious look in the eyes of the two men and the woman instantly changed to deep sympathy and sorrow. Particularly did the eyes of the man in civilian clothes change. They softened instantly and admiration crept into their depths. At once Combat was sure of what he had suspected when he first saw the man. He was either Polish Intelligence or Secret Police.

"Ah yes, we all read of that, Mr. Combat," the military officer murmured. "The swine! But you said it was two days ago?

It was five days ago. This is now Sunday. You have been here in the hospital for two days. You...."

A DULL booming and rumbling sound from somewhere in the distance cut off the officer's words. Rage leaped into his eyes and the knuckles of his bronzed hands gripping the end of the bed showed white through the skin.

"Let them come, the dogs!" he cried in a ringing voice. "Poland will fight to the last man, to the last drop of blood. Hitler has started it, but Poland will finish it, by God!"

Combat started up in the bed and hardly felt the stab of pain through the back of his neck.

"Hitler has marched?" he cried.

"Friday night the first of his troops crossed the frontier," the other said. "But of course you don't know, do you? This morning England and France declared war on Germany. Yes, it has come again. The world is at war once more."

Combat slowly laid back on the pillow as the truth hammered around and around inside his brain. True, he had known that war was inevitable, but it was a shock to learn that it had all begun while he was unconscious in a hospital cot. It maddened him. He felt that the gods had cheated him. He should be in England now, rejoining his former R.A.F. squadron. Whipping himself into shape for the real thing. He....

Suddenly complete memory of what had happened came rushing back like flood waters pouring through a broken dam. Uncle Harry! Pinneberg, and Heinrich Staube! Agent Sixteen, and 'Mons'! The British blockade to be futile against U-boats.

A secret German radio wave that could explode mines at great distances! Staube… Staube… Staube!

The name pounded against his brain, and the weariness of mind and body that he had first felt upon regaining consciousness was wiped away. Strength flowed back into his body and the blood surged through his veins. He sat up in bed and scowled the nurse away when she started to restrain him.

"Hell's bells!" he exploded. "Bed is no place for me! Where are my clothes? Get them, somebody!"

"Mr. Combat, please!" the military police officer said sharply. "The wound is not bad, not deep, but you lost considerable blood. You should remain in the hospital for a few days."

"Not me, sir!" Combat said. "I've got things to do!"

"What, may I ask?" the other said.

Combat gave him a quick look, and then smiled grimly. "Twice I've been shot at for being something I wasn't!" he clipped out. "Now, by God, I'm really going to work!" Combat suddenly turned and jabbed a stiff finger at the man in civilian clothes. "You're Polish Intelligence aren't you?" he asked quickly.

The civilian hesitated a brief moment and then nodded.

"Did you ever work with the British?" Combat demanded.

"I helped Lord Brainbridge a lot, I hope," the Pole said with an unmistakable ring in his voice.

Combat grinned. "Now we're getting places!" he cried, and beckoned to the man. "Come here. Excuse us a moment, please."

As the nurse and the military police officer stepped back with undecided frowns on their faces, Combat pulled the civilian down until his lips were to the man's ear.

"Mons," he whispered softly.

The civilian stiffened as though shot. Then he straightened up and his dark face was wreathed in smiles.

"So!" he cried. "Then that explains a lot. Permit me to place myself at your service, sir."

"First help me get my clothes," Combat grinned. "Then take me some place where we can talk… and not get shot."

"Both are as good as done!" the other said eagerly.

CHAPTER 9
PHANTOM WINGS

NIGHT HUNG dark and brooding over eastern Poland. To the west and southwest there was a faint glow of crimson and yellow, low down. Every now and then the glow grew brighter, and then faded down again. The glow was from war flames licking at the frontier villages, and when it increased it did so because German artillery shells had found a new house, or a new ammo dump.

It was Monday night, October the second. Hitler had been hammering at Poland for three days and his swastika-branded killers were sweeping relentlessly forward, like a tidal wave of flame, despite the valiant efforts of the Poles to stem the advance. It was steel might against blood courage, and the gods were already recording the results in their ledgers of time. Even the bravest heart can be stopped by a bullet. Poland was doomed. Hitler knew it, the world knew it, and even the Poles must have known it deep down in their hearts. Perhaps someday they would be restored to independence, but for a while the Nazis would crawl all over their country like vermin. And it was in the cards that the Moscow grubs would partake of their share of the blood feast, too.

Nosing a powerful Heinkel ship skyward over Posen, Bill Combat stared at that red glow on the horizon, thought of all those things, and groaned through clenched teeth helplessly. Three precious days had been lost forever, as far as he was concerned. Last Friday there had been no war between England and Germany, and he might have been able to travel to Pinneberg unmolested. True, there would be a dangerous side to his reentering Germany. The Gestapo might have maintained a watch in case he *did* return. He was a spy. Yes, a self-elected spy. A spy without authorization, you might say. But it made little difference. He was heading back into enemy country now. And what was more; he was doing it in an enemy plane, and wearing the uniform of an enemy pilot.

For those two items he had to thank one Rennard Passake, of Polish Intelligence. From the hospital Passake had taken him to a spot where they could talk undisturbed. There Combat had told Passake that he wished to return into Germany. He had admitted that such had been Lord Brainbridge's request, but he had not told Passake what part of Germany he wished to visit, nor why. The dead Brainbridge's warning still rang in Combat's ears. "Trust no one." Combat had followed that advice to the letter. He had told Passake just enough to get the man's complete cooperation, but nothing that would give the Pole an inkling of where he was going, or what he intended to do when he got there.

And be it said for Rennard Passake, he had not asked embarrassing questions. He had simply done as Combat asked, and had been both eager and pleased to be of service. Passake had obtained a Nazi lieutenant's uniform for Combat, and a flying suit, helmet and goggles—and perhaps most important of all, a German made Heinkel plane, sold to Poland several months ago. From its wings and fuselage the Polish Flying Corps insignia had been removed and the Nazi emblems substituted instead.

All that had required a certain amount of time. Only twenty minutes ago Combat had gripped Passake's hand in thanks and farewell and climbed into the pit of the Heinkel, in a small and half-hidden field a few miles north of Posen. And now he was climbing the ship for altitude and the protection of the low hanging clouds, but heading directly south in case Passake or anybody else in Posen was watching him.

When finally the altimeter quivered at the fifteen thousand foot mark and all about him was darkness, he throttled the engine considerably and coasted around until he was on a compass course to the northwest. Still climbing a little, he held the stick with his knees and drew a thin flat book from his pocket. For a moment he fingered it in almost a caressing sort of manner. Then he deliberately tore it into small pieces. Shoving forward the triplex glass cockpit cowling, he stuck his hand out and let the prop-wash pull the torn pieces from his hand and swirl them off into oblivion. The torn pieces were all that was left of his American passport. He turned in the seat and watched the last bits fly away.

"So long," he grunted.

HE TURNED front and dismissed all thoughts from his mind save those that had to do with the task ahead. Heinrich Staube, in Pinneberg, was his goal. A four hour flight lay before him, and what happened at the end was in the lap of the gods. Perhaps there was some better way to reach Pinneberg unobserved, but he had considered every possible method he could think of, and had decided that flight in a German plane as a German pilot was the best bet.

Once he was clear of Poland he would have nothing to worry about in the air. Ground detectors would recognize the sound of his German engine at once. As a matter of fact he was flying high, now, simply to avoid any Polish planes that might be in the air, and to keep out of sight of Polish archie batteries. Once over Germany he would come lower and be perfectly willing for Nazi searchlights to pick him up.

But arrival at Pinneberg? That would be something else. Luckily he had done considerable flying over the Hamburg sector and knew the terrain well. Finding Pinneberg would not be too difficult even in a blackout. There were several flying fields, as well as seaplane basins about that section, and any one of them would suit his purpose.

"Right!" he grunted the rest of his thoughts aloud. "I'll just pick out one of them and make a crash landing. There's no means of identification on me, and so while I have a lapse of memory and act dumb from the crash, the Nazi rats can scratch their heads about me. Beginning with then, I'll simply keep on the alert for the next break. Yeah, a few days of rest in the Pinneberg Naval Hospital might be just the kind of a break I need."

His plan of action suddenly seemed to appear less than perfect, and a clammy chill rippled through him and he shivered slightly in spite of himself. Germany at peace was more or less of a steel trap to those who hated Nazism. Germany at war would be doubly difficult to fool. Yet....

"You've got a job, guy!" he grated to himself aloud. "Find Staube. That's more important than any other job you could do for England right now."

Beating back the tiny voice of indecision and warning within him, he roared over the Polish border, then deliberately came down to ten thousand feet or so and continued onward. Every so often he checked ground lights with the map in the cockpit and held to his course. Once or twice he snapped on the two-way radio, but the constant twanging buzz in the earphones caused him to give it up. But it did give him food for frowning thought. Some powerful German station was jamming the air so that nothing could go through.

He wondered a lot about that, and little by little he convinced himself that it was but for one purpose. The Germans were jamming the air so that Poland had no radio contact with the outside world. It was a stupid idea, but typical of Nazis thoroughness. So long as the outside world had no definite word of how Hitler's march was progressing, then that much better it was for Hitler's troops. Their mistakes and blunders would be discovered too late to make any difference. They....

He let the rest trail off as he absently snapped on the radio again. The sound was different. True, it was continuous and seemingly unending, but decidedly different in note. It was more like the whining roar of an electric train rushing down a long tunnel. Either that, or like a hundred dynamos running slightly off center. For several moments the sound held him fascinated, and he was suddenly dead sure that it was not any radio-jamming signal. If he did not know he was in the air, he could have closed his eyes and sworn that he stood inside some huge electric powerhouse.

Suddenly a wild note of stark warning ripped through him. It was as though his sixth sense had taken complete charge of his brain. Hardly realizing it, he twisted sharply around in the seat and stared back. He stiffened, gasped a curse, and impulsively rubbed his free hand across his eyes. But there wasn't anything the matter with his eyes. *He could still see it!* He could see a swarm of dark clouds, blacker than the night, hurtling straight toward him.

A nocturnal mirage? Had he gone crazy, and was he seeing things in his warped imagination? Had that Mauser rifle bullet done something to his brain after all? Those and hundreds of other dizzy questions zipped through his head, and then he yelled wildly, kicked hard on the right rudder pedal, and hurled the stick over. The violent maneuver of the powerful, fast plane made his eyeballs try to roll backwards in their sockets, and the turning force of the plane tried to draw every drop of blood out of his head and arms and legs. For a few seconds he was in a world of shimmering white, and there was a terrific burning sensation in his lungs.

THEN SUDDENLY the thousands of invisible hands that seemed to grip all parts of his body let go, and he became conscious of the fact he was spinning furiously earthward. Even as that realization came to him the plane went skidding off, crazily to the side like a leaf or a scrap of paper caught in a sudden draft of air. A whirring roar filled his ears and without reason he thought of the time, when, as a child, he had stood too close to the edge of a railroad station platform and his mother had snatched him back as an express howled past. He'd never forgotten those horrible seconds of bellowing thunder, and as he struggled to regain control of his gyrating Heinkel, memory came back as though the event were actually being repeated.

Cursing and shouting aloud, he battled the ship back onto even keel, noted that he'd lost a good thousand feet, and then froze still in the seat as he glanced upward. There above him, seeming so close that he could almost reach up and touch it, was a vast expanse of airplane wing. Never in all of his aeronautical travels had he ever seen anything like it. It was faint and almost extinct in the darkness of the heavens. But because he was so close to it, he could make out its outline and be sure that it was not just a stray stratum of cloud scud being whipped along by the wind. No, not that. It was a gigantic monoplane wing. A huge wing with no nose nor fuselage, nor tail. Just a mighty phantom wing sweeping away from him at terrific speed.

Unconsciously he blinked his eyes and stared again. This time he was able to make out other moving shapes that rushed along with the one strange wing he had seen, as though the lot were tied together. A cluster of phantom-winged giants rushing along up the Elbe toward Hamburg and the North Sea! Even as he blinked again, the strange night air armada was gone. It had blended in completely with the black skies and was lost to his view. A weird, unbelievable sky armada. Not a light showing, and but for instinctive flying on his part it would have thundered into him. The thought filled his body with shudders. Against that on-rushing phantom thing of the air, his all-metal Heinkel would have offered as much resistance as a rowing shell against the prow of the steamship *Queen Mary*.

"It couldn't have been planes!" he muttered in an awed voice. "Hell, they *couldn't* have been. They don't make them that big. I must be going nuts. Yet, so help me God, the one I did see had a monoplane wing. A high wing monoplane job or I'm crazy."

The sound of his own voice seemed to act as a release spring for his tightened muscles. He belted his free hand against the throttle, opened up the Benz wide and whipped around in pursuit. Hunched forward in the seat, he strained his eyes ahead for another glimpse of the blood-chilling cavalcade of night wings. But he was unable to see anything, and for no particular reason he snapped on the two-way radio. The strange sound filled the ear phones no longer. As a matter of fact it was with a start he heard a man's voice speaking in English.

"… *although the list of the Athenia's victims is not yet complete it is feared that when all the boats carrying the torpedoed ship's survivors reach port the total number lost will be in the neighborhood of one thousand. A late report received from Berlin denies that the Athenia was sunk by a submarine. The German Admiralty claims that there were no U-boats in those waters. I now return you to NBC in New York. This is London saying good night."*

The back of Combat's neck crawled as the set went silent. It gave him an eerie feeling to be flying high over Germany and suddenly tune in on a short-wave broadcast from London to New York. So the Athenia had been sunk? He and his mother had crossed on her from Montreal on their last visit to England. A passenger ship she was, and the Nazis had sunk her? Let the rats deny to hell and back that a U-boat hadn't done it. He, for one, wouldn't believe it. He....

He caught his breath with a sharp gasp as a sudden thought came to him.

"That secret German wave that can explode mines!" he whispered. "Could bombs have been placed aboard the Athenia, and the Germans set them off by radio wave? God, I wonder."

All the time he had been listening to the news broadcast and mulling over its significance, one half of his attention had been steadfastly fixed on the broad expanse of black sky ahead. But he did not see a single sign of the weird spectacle that had made him hurtle the Heinkel earthward from out of the path of an onrushing phantom juggernaut. It had vanished in the night as mysteriously as it had appeared before his startled eyes.

Memory of it still chilling his heart a bit, he stared down over the side, picked up the cluster of lights from a few towns, spotted them on his map, and realized that he should be seeing the twist of the Elbe at Hamburg very shortly.

"I must have been seeing things," he forced himself to admit aloud as he straightened up and gazed forward again. "I've stayed at the same altitude, and if there's anything that can run away that fast from this Heinkel, damned if I won't eat it. I... My God, what's that?"

The faint flow of lights that he took for Hamburg appeared up over the lip of the horizon ahead. But as he stared at them they went out as though some giant had drawn a huge blanket over the top of the city. But they didn't stay out! The lights nearest him began to appear again, and in the next second he knew what caused it. Something was passing through the air between his plane and the lights on the horizon. Something below his altitude. Something! Giant wings that seemed to spread out a mile in length. One... two... three... *four!*

Four great shapes moving over the Elbe ahead and below him and blotting out huge patches of Hamburg. A moment later he lost them completely. Lost them because the entire water front of Hamburg was suddenly blacked out. And then, without warning, savage, rattling death came chopping down on him from above, threatening to smash him from the sky with its fury.

CHAPTER 10
MIDNIGHT FURY

IN THE next split second Bill Combat became a whirlwind of furious action. No sooner had the yammering of the shots cracked against his ears than he hurled his Heinkel off to the left, cut back in again and then pulled the nose up in a roaring power zoom for altitude. Then and then only did he take time out to glance around for signs of his attacker. He spotted twin streams of jetting flame off to his left and still somewhat *above* him, and by following the jetting flame back to its source; he was able to make out the blurred shape of wings and a fuselage.

The quick flash of the plane's outline caused him to believe that it was another Heinkel interceptor. He gulped with momentary relief. If that ship were one of the new Nazi Messerschmitts, he was in for a lot of trouble, if not death. The monoplane Messerschmitt was the fastest thing on military wings. True, its great superiority was in its tremendous speed, well over three hundred miles per hour, rather than in its maneuverability. But dog fighting in the dark is far different than in daylight. While he groped about trying to bring a Messerschmitt into his sights the faster craft could zoom for heaven, spin over, and come down in a burst of speed that would make a haywire comet look slow.

"But even if it is a Messerschmitt!" he grated aloud and yanked back the loading handles of his guns, "the lad's going to have something to remember, by God." He smiled tightly.

With a grim nod for emphasis, he spun his Heinkel around on a wingtip and charged straight up at the other plane. He fired both guns and "see-sawed" the nose so as to scatter his shots over a wide area. In the bad light it was practically impossible to get the fast-flying ship in his sights, and so until he had gained the other's altitude he had to "spread" his bursts and trust to lucky bullets finding their mark.

None did, however, though he did gain one objective. His bursts evidently came too close for comfort because the other plane suddenly whipped out of its dive and went banging down and around to the left. In the split seconds allowed, Combat gained the precious altitude he needed, then hunched forward over the stick and peered hard down across the black sky at the other plane. In the matter of a few seconds he knew beyond all doubt that it was a Heinkel and not a Messerschmitt.

"Fair enough!" he bellowed and closed in on the ship. "Not that it matters a hell of a lot, though. I'll...."

The rest never left his lips. At that moment he suddenly saw something that made him completely forget the other ship in the air. Far below him, a weird purple glow had spread over a section of the Hamburg water front. It made him think of the glow cast by the lights used for night work in print shops and factories. He stared down at it, and then realized with a jerk that the glow seemed to come from three or four grotesque shadows floating on the waters of the Elbe. And in almost the same instant those shadows took on the definite shapes of giant monoplane wings.

"But there are no bodies to the ships!" he gasped aloud. "Just giant flying wings, that's what they are. Pterodactyl designed ships with no tails, or I'm nuts! And the Nazis have been experimenting along the pterodactyl lines? Hell, I didn't even get as much as a hint of *that*. I...U-boats! I'll be damned!"

As he yelled the last, he hunched way forward as though in doing so he could bring the weird scene below closer to his eyes. And as he did he unconsciously dipped the nose and started losing his precious altitude at close to three hundred miles an hour. But for the second he didn't give that important item a single thought. Between the huge wings floating on the Elbe, he could make out the steel-plated cigars that were German U-boats. And he could even see the tiny figures of men who seemed to be racing over short catwalks that joined the subs with the floating wings.

AND THEN he no longer had the chance for a better inspection. A ring of archie batteries started hurling barking death up into his face. And the other plane that was now above him once more came roaring down with both guns hammering out close to fifteen hundred shots a minute each.

Cursing himself for his forgetful stupidity, he yanked his Heinkel out of its dive and went cutting away through a sky filled with hissing and whining doom. He heard a few pieces of shrapnel bang into the metal cowling of his plane and go twanging off into space. Then a burst from the other ship's guns smacked against the forward section of his glass cockpit cowling and instantly transformed the clear, three-layer glass into a crazy crisscross pattern of thousands of tiny white cracks.

His heart leaped up to clog his throat. Another burst where that one had struck and he'd get a bellyful of hot, nickel-jacketed lead. And there was no doubt in his mind now why he had been suddenly and mysteriously attacked. At the start he had thought that Lady Luck was simply laughing in his face again; that he had been followed from Posen and attacked; that the chase which had been started way back at the Tempelhof Airport was simply being continued.

Now, though, he realized that was not so. Not knowing it, he had blundered over forbidden territory. A patrolling plane had spotted him, and its pilot had come down to wipe him from the sky, regardless of whether he was friend or enemy. If that were not the case, he would at least have been signaled to land and identify himself. He had not been given that opportunity, however. He had flown into restricted air. He had followed a weird night armada to its nest, and for his curiosity he had been marked for death.

The last brought a thin grin to his lips. He whipped the Heinkel into a full roll, stalled it for a brief instant as he came out, then slashed off and around to the right. As he did, a savage burst originally aimed at his cockpit twanged harmlessly into the metal tail and lost itself in the night.

The attacking ship, looking like a gray ghost in the reflection of the weird light cast up from the waters of the Elbe, started to race off into the clear. Its pilot leaned on the controls a split second too late. Both guns blazing, Combat raked the craft from its spinning prop all the way back to the tail. He had the savage satisfaction of seeing the plane jerk sidewise in the air as though it had glanced off an invisible brick wall.

However, if he thought that was the end, he was sorely disappointed in the next second. In a flash the German pilot righted his craft and whipped around to come gun-blazing in again. The Nazi was tough, or at least the gods of battle had shied all slugs from Combat's guns away from his hide. Guns spitting flame, the plane bored in at rocket speed, and for a brief instant Combat stared death right in the face. But only for a brief second, however. Back came the stick into his stomach, and the Heinkel bucked and quivered as though unable to respond in time. And then its nose shot up and it tore straight for heaven at terrific speed. The twanging sound of bullets smacking against his ship ceased and Combat gulped out the air that had been locked in his aching lungs.

"God, am I rusty at this sort of thing!" he gasped and flattened off the top of the zoom. "I should have nailed him cold when I had such a swell chance. Snap out of it, guy, or you're going to be just a waste of time to everybody!"

Echoing his words with a curse, he started hurling his Heinkel all over the sky in a desperate effort to stay clear of the Nazi's guns. With each passing split second his heart strings became tauter and cold sweat oozed out on his forehead and trickled down into his eyes. It was as though his bursts had suddenly snapped the Nazi pilot into the realization that the scrap was no game—that it was for keeps. At any rate, the Nazi had suddenly started flying like a madman. His ship seemed to be every place at the same time. And although Combat yammered his guns time and time again, the other plane always seemed to dart out into the clear in the nick of time.

"The rat's good!" he breathed hoarsely. "And I can't keep this up all night. They may send another louse up to help him, and then it *will* be curtains!"

HIS WHOLE body aching from the terrific strain of hurling the fast Heinkel all over the sky, he cursed himself onto greater effort and practically flew the wings off the plane. But it got results and hope began to pound through him. Little by little the other pilot ceased to fly so recklessly. Little by little he went over on the defensive. And the instant he did, Combat leaped in to take full advantage of the slight opportunity offered.

And then, as he started crowding the Nazi plane earthward, he realized that the weird purple glow below was growing fainter and fainter. It was as though the war gods had now decided to play him the dirty trick of blacking out everything so he'd be unable to see his antagonist. In short, unless he got his man in the next few seconds, he'd never get him at all. Not that shooting down the other ship would gain him any particular advantage. Now that the fight had taken place, his original idea of crash-landing on some field and acting dumb was knocked into a cocked hat. They would only have to take a look at his bullet-riddled plane to know he had been scrapping. And then, when they started asking questions....

"Being dumb won't help!" he growled. "Ten to one I'd get the firing squad for having blundered over a restricted area in the first place. But the hell with that. Getting this rat is the thing I want to do first, and how!"

The last was but a hint of what really was in his brain. For a far greater reason than his own safety did he want to bring down that Heinkel that yammered about him. This was the first air battle he had ever engaged in. The affair over the Polish border had not been one exactly, for the sport job had not been equipped with guns. But he had guns, now, and there was a damn German in the night sky. German airmen had sent his father to death. German airmen had snuffed out the life of his dear mother. He wasn't fighting for England, or France, or any country right now. He was just plain Bill Combat, the avenger of the family name. This was his first chance to pay back for something that would never be settled in full until there were no longer any swastika vultures on the wing.

Lower and lower dimmed the weird purple glow on the waters of the Elbe below. But he paid no attention to that. His eyes were fastened on the other Heinkel, twisting and turning in the air about him. And with lips drawn back flat against his teeth, he cursed and booted his own ship around after it. Suddenly the other craft went into a crazy spin and a cry of joy rose to Combat's lips. Had he nailed the rat at last? Had the last burst ripped through the glass cockpit cowling?

But no! The Nazi was simply trying the old fake spinning trick in a desperate effort to quit the fight and make good his mistake while there was time. Instantly Combat sliced his own plane into a spin and followed the other down.

"Not a chance, louse!" he howled. "Not a chance!"

Hardly had the last left his lips when the other plane suddenly whipped out of its spin and started scooting away. In a flash Combat was out of his own spin and after it. However, the Nazi plane had picked up a quarter of a mile, and for one hellish second Combat thought that his cause was lost. The sky was getting darker than ever and both planes being of the same make, it was doubtful if he could overhaul the other before it was too late.

But the curse on his lips died unspoken. Rather, it changed into a wild crazy yell of savage excitement. The Nazi had suddenly banked sharply. The plane split-arced around and came rushing straight at him, guns blazing. Instinctively Combat ducked in the pit, then he immediately cursed his action, straightened up, and held his own ship steady, firing both guns.

NOSE TO nose rushed the two planes through the fast-fading light. Nickel-jacketed lead bounced and twanged off the nose of Combat's plane. The glass cockpit cowling became a mass of white cracks, but he didn't so much as change his direction a hair. It was more than a matter of marksmanship now. It was courage. Guts! Somebody had to give air or two bullet-spitting wasps would hurtle straight into each other and go swirling down into hell in a blaze of flame. German courage against Yank courage. One had to break—and break damn fast—or the grim reaper would be the only winner.

Like a statue of stone, Combat sat hunched over the stick, his eyes glued to the whirling propeller of the other Heinkel that rushed closer and closer. For one brief instant, because he was human after all, cold chill gripped his heart and he was filled with the almost overpowering impulse to twist off and away. But the impulse was killed in his brain even as it was born. He simply tightened his grip on the stick and pressed harder against the trigger trips.

A hundred yards away from that on-rushing Heinkel! Fifty yards away! Twenty-five! Combat saw his bullets chewing and clawing their way into the nose of the ship. And in an abstract sort of way he was conscious of bullets banging and slamming into his own plane. Twenty yards… ten… five….

"To hell with you!" Combat screamed.

"I'm holding! We'll see who quits!"

And it was in that second that the courage, guts, and what

it takes in the pinches, folded up. It folded up in a Nazi heart. Up went the nose of the on-rushing Heinkel, and instinctively Combat closed his eyes and waited for his own prop, to claw into the belly of the zooming plane. But no violent crash hurled him up against the instrument board, and no ungodly sounds of ripping and tearing metal filled his ears. He opened his eyes to find himself still thundering forward on an even keel, and the other Heinkel zooming wildly skyward above him.

"Can't take it, eh, louse?" Combat yelled and hauled back on the stick. "Well, here's something you've *got* to take."

The last word was punctuated by Combat's guns. The zooming Heinkel suddenly staggered sidewise in the air, and for a brief moment it hovered almost motionless in the sky. Then slowly it fell over on one wing. A tiny tongue of flame licked out from beneath its engine cowling, and the flame grew bigger and brighter. Then, suddenly, what had but a few moments ago been a bullet-spitting Heinkel became a roaring ball of flame hurtling straight down toward the waters of the Elbe.

A savage, joyous shout sprang from Combat's lips, but it was almost instantly cut off by a sharp cry of alarm. The controls had suddenly gone mushy in his grasp, and his Heinkel was flip-flopping about in the now black sky, touched only by the flames of the falling plane.

Impulsively he reached forward and snapped off the ignition and yanked back the throttle. That done with, his hand streaked to the adjustable tail-plane lever, but working it helped very little. Bullet-nicked control rods had finally given way under the terrific strain of maneuvers, and now he was sliding downward in the wake of his victim. Try as he might, his battling of the controls did little if any good. A harsh bitter laugh spilled from his lips as he realized the full significance of the situation. He had won, yes. But what good had it done him?

Down there below him was a dead Nazi; killed by bullets from his own guns. But maybe it was a tie after all. The Nazi's bullets had done their job, too. He was falling helplessly downward… into what? The odds were all in favor of a crash that would snuff out his life just as quickly as those flames had snuffed out the Nazi pilot's life!

"But not without a fight!" he grated and struggled anew to get the plane under control.

CHAPTER 11
SAILOR'S GRAVE

A HUNDRED lifetimes seemed to drag past Bill Combat's eyes. Through a blur he saw the flaming Heinkel drop lower and lower against the curtain of earth, and water below. And then, just as it was about to strike, the glow of the flames lighted up an object below. Combat stared frozen completely forgetful of his own immediate fate. The Heinkel was dropping straight down on one of the weird pterodactyl shaped wings resting on the surface of the water. He had just time enough in which to catch a glimpse of a German U-boat seemingly moored to the odd shaped wing. Then the flaming Heinkel struck.

A flash of red flame, a momentary fountain of burning

embers, and then all hell spewed up from the waters of the Elbe. A world of flashing purple light engulfed Combat's flip-flopping plane. Giant hands seemed to reach up and grab hold of his craft. For a long second he was held motionless in skies composed of blinding purple light. And then, as though mighty coiled steel springs had been released, he was flung far out across the world.

His brain hammered and his ears rang with sound. Hardly conscious of doing so, he clung with both hands to the joystick, hauled it back into his stomach and automatically braced himself in the seat. Like a card skidded into a cyclone he and his plane went spinning end over end through an eternity of sound and crazy colored light. His muscles seemed to freeze stiff, and his brain was completely devoid of all thought or sensation.

A minute—an hour—a year? He had no way of telling how long it lasted. As a matter of fact he didn't even try to gauge the time. His brain was too stunned, the cells too clogged by the roaring rush to nowhere. Eventually, though, he was able to grasp the realization that the flashing purple light was gone. All about him was inky darkness. Even the crazy gyrations of the plane had stopped. A crazy sensation came to him that he was floating upside down on a softly whispering black cloud. Floating upside down, because enough of his senses started functioning again to tell him that he was hanging, head down, on his safety belt harness—a hell of a fix to be in!

Gulping air into his burning lungs he forced the stick over, managed somehow to reach the rudder pedal with one foot. Perhaps part of the controls held together long enough to cause the plane to twist over onto level keel, with the nose slightly dipped earthward. Or perhaps it was simply a crazy, sudden cross current of air that accomplished his wish for him.

At any rate he came right side up. And, not a split second too soon, either. Even as he tried to bring his burning eyes into focus on the blanket of darkness ahead, the plane hit something belly first, seemed to shake every joint in his body loose, and went ricocheting off and upward. A split second later, it dropped and hit again. Cold spray whipped back through his half-opened cockpit cowling, and it was then that he knew!

Lady Luck had smiled upon him after all. The belly of his half-stalling ship had smacked at an angle against water. The wheels, being cranked up into the wings, gave the belly a smooth surface, like the underside of a surf board. And his gliding angle had been so shallow the nose had not bit into the water. He'd struck it flat on his ship's belly, glanced off up into the air for a bit and then stalled back onto the water again.

He imagined that he had landed somewhere in the Elbe, but whether it was above or below the port of Hamburg he did not know. It was impossible to determine anything in the world of inky darkness all around him. Not a light showed anyplace. There was hardly any sound, save the slap-slap of stiff, wind-blown waves hitting against his wing and fuselage—then, a sudden lurch downward by the nose of the plane cut short his wondering.

The bullet-riddled plane was taking water fast. In a few minutes It would sink beneath him, and carry him down with it unless he got himself free. Thought and action became one.

He quickly unsnapped his safety belt harness, slammed the shattered cowling all the way forward and stood up on the seat. The nose along with half of the wing was already under water. The tail was slowly pointing skyward as the Heinkel poised itself for its final plunge down into the depths.

Panting from the effort, he tore off his heavy flying suit and dragged off his German field boots. Next he ripped off his tunic, balanced himself on the cockpit rim, and then dived. Even as he dived, the doomed Heinkel seemed to drop away from under him, and so, instead of cleaving the water sharp, like a knife, he stumbled and hit it in a belly-whopper that made every square inch of his skin smart with stinging pain, from his toes up to his forehead.

HE RAISED his head; shook the water from his face, then swam forward a few strokes. He treaded water, turned around and peered hopefully about in the shadowy darkness for some piece of the plane's wreckage to which he could cling. There were a few bits floating about, but nothing that would give him any support when he tired of swimming. He realized bitterly that the metal Heinkel was on the bottom, fathoms below him.

"And where am I?" he muttered. "Yeah, where *am* I? Right in the middle of nothing. Pick your direction, guy… and *maybe* you will be heading for shore!"

He laughed dryly at the humor of the situation. All he knew was that he was treading water in the middle of nowhere. Perhaps firm ground was fifty yards away and he could reach it without much effort. And then, again, he might be out in the open reaches of the North Sea. It was as funny as it was serious.

But the humor did not last for long in his brain. The water had soaked through the few clothes he had left on, and even in the middle of summer, the waters up around the northern coast of Germany are not any too warm. This would not be fun.

"Better swim if only to keep warm!" he muttered through chattering teeth. "Yeah, just start swimming straight ahead as I am. It's as good as any direction to pick."

He started propelling himself through the water with a long easy side arm stroke. Little by little his swimming drove the cold from his body. Minutes passed, one piling on top of the next. More minutes and still more. And finally, all that had happened began to take its toll in his strength. He swam more slowly, and treaded water to rest more often. And each time he stopped swimming the cold attacked his limbs more punishingly than ever. And all the time he seemed to remain in a limitless expanse of water with no boundaries and no horizons.

Little stabs of fear started darting through his brain. He was a fool to think he could keep this up until daybreak. There wasn't a single thread of light in the sky. Not a sign to tell him which direction was east. And even if he did last until daylight, what then? The chances were that he'd probably find himself surrounded by water clear to the four horizons. He could still be in the Elbe and unable to see either shore. The ninety mile river that led from the North Sea, up past the Kiel Canal to Hamburg, was no little brook by any manner of means.

"And its current is probably taking me right down the middle of the damn thing, if I am in it!" he breathed. "Hell, I've…."

A tiny wave slapping against his half opened mouth helped

to stop the rest. But what really caused him to cut short his voice was a sense of vibrating movement somewhere in the water about him. He could hear nothing, and actually he could feel nothing. It was merely that part of his brain suddenly became tuned to a peculiar movement of vibration, just as the detector tube of a radio set becomes tuned to the pulsations of an ether wave.

He stopped swimming, floated like a man drowned, but every one of his senses strained to pin down the sensation and translate it into something definite. And then suddenly it all became very clear to him. No, not that he had figured it out himself. Rather it was the muffled sound of a voice; a voice speaking in German off to his right and in back of him a little. He didn't quite get the meaning of the words. Then after a moment of silence the voice spoke again. This time it seemed no more than ten yards from where he floated in the water.

"Turn on the bow searchlights! There's wreckage in the water. Stop engines or we may foul the propeller!"

Combat parted his numbed lips to cry out, but closed them again before he had made a sound. There was a boat close to him, but it was a German craft obviously. What good would it do him to be pulled from the inky waters by German hands? What...?

Before he could battle the problem out in his own mind the whole thing was settled for him. A shaft of light cut the night air like a thin yellow blade. It swung across the water to the left, stopped and swung back the other way. In the next second Combat was blinking into its dazzling brilliance. A voice yelled hoarsely behind it.

"Man in water off the port bow! Helm to port! Hold her as she goes. Deck watch, man the life line! Get a move on, you *schweinehunds!*"

For one mad moment Combat had the wild impulse to slip down below the surface of the water and swim away from the disc of light that held him pinned fast. But before he could do that his hands treading water suddenly struck against cold steel plates. The beam of the searchlight seemed to burn right through his blinded eyes into the back of his brain. In the next moment a loop of line settled over his head and shoulders with a splash.

The line was drawn taut about him and he was pulled closer to the cold steel plates. Then strong hands reached down out of the circle of light, gripped hold of him and lifted him clear of the water.

"Take him below!" a voice ordered. "Kill that searchlight. It's just a bit of airplane wreckage. Half speed ahead!"

Still more or less blinded by the light, and hardly able to remain on his feet, Combat let himself be lead forward along a curving steel deck and then up a short companionway ladder. By then, shadowy objects began to take shape before his aching eyes. When he reached the top of that companionway ladder he knew that he had been pulled from the water by the crew of a German U-boat. Truth sent icy chills slicing through his heart. God, how far had he swum in the water? Had his plane been sighted when it fell into the water, and this U-boat been sent down the Elbe to pick him up?

THE QUESTION burned through his brain as two ruddy faced sailors helped him down the conning tower companionway into the innards of the submarine. At the first deck landing he was brought to a halt. A hatchet faced, flint-eyed German Navy commander confronted him and fixed him with a steady gaze. From a long ways off, Combat heard his own voice speak.

"I owe you my life, *Herr* Commander," he said. "That swine, the one I was ordered to shoot down, he died, yes?"

The sudden look of amazement in the U-boat commander's face made Combat realize that his subconscious brain had caused his lips to say the right thing. And that he had done so was doubly made certain a split second later when the U-boat officer spoke.

"*Himmel,* so it is you we have picked up, and not that blundering fool?" the German gasped. "It was his plane and not yours that fell into the mooring basin, eh? But, *Gott,* that was two hours ago! And we find you here over twenty miles from Hamburg? *Himmel,* it is almost unbelievable!"

It seemed almost unbelievable to Combat, too, that he had been plucked from the water so far from Hamburg. But when he thought of that tremendous purple flame explosion, and of how his plane had been sent spinning endlessly across the heavens, twenty miles seemed no distance at all. But he didn't give it much thought. By a blind bit of luck he had established an identity that made him safe from the German U-boat crew at least. They took him for the patrolling pilot, and... and thank God for that.

"The swine was killed, eh, *Herr* Commander?" he muttered through water swelled lips.

The anger that suddenly leaped into the U-boat officer's face both—alarmed and mystified Combat.

"Dead, and it serves the blundering fool right!" the German clipped. "But he damn near killed many of us, and no thanks to *you* Lieutenant, whatever your name is! He struck one of the magnet planes just as they were making fast to one of our boats. Contact was broken and it was a miracle the whole basin wasn't burned to a crisp. *Gott*, as it was, the voltage shock almost blew our bow out of water. No, you will receive no medal for this night's work, my flying friend. You will be lucky, no matter what punishment they give you. Take him to the officers' ward-room. Get him warm clothes and something to drink. I must radio Hamburg."

The last the U-boat commander spoke to the two sailors holding onto Combat. Then, flashing Combat a quick angry look, the German turned on his heel and walked aft. Combat shrugged, tried to appear politely annoyed by the German's gesture and then allowed the sailors to lead him forward to the officers' wardroom. But he did not feel annoyed in the least. On the contrary he felt no little alarmed. Evidently he had come close to creating a disaster of major proportions in the Hamburg basin. Punishment was in store for him. That didn't bother him much. What did bother him was that should the U-boat commander return him to the Hamburg naval author-ities, it would be soon learned that he was not the pilot who had been aloft on patrol. And then....

"Escape from this U-boat!" His brain flashed the warning as he started peeling the water logged clothes from his weary body.

CHAPTER 12
DEATH PUTS TO SEA

I T SEEMED to Combat that he had no sooner climbed into warm seaman's clothing and gulped down a whole glass of stomach warming schnapps, than the U-boat's commander entered the wardroom. The captain's lips were curled in a faint grin, but the grin was not shared by his eyes. They bored into Combat's and the Yank suspected that it was smug, almost triumphant satisfaction he saw in their slate grey depths.

"You are lucky, *Lieutenant* Schmidt," the commander grunted and poured himself a drink. "Whatever punishment they plan for your stupidity in shooting down that fool right into the basin, and nearly killing us all, is to be postponed for a little while anyway. You are a good sailor, eh?"

"Why?" Combat asked absently.

"We may meet some rough water out there," the other said and jerked a thumb over his shoulder. "We've got to run under the swine British blockade now. But for your foolish action the magnet planes would have us safely at sea. Yet, I do not mind. That's what a submarine is made for eh? To go under the water, not over it!"

The German laughed at what seemed to him to be quite a joke. Combat joined in the laugh, but not because he had found anything funny in the other's words, but simply to cover up his own feelings. Some of them were relieved that the U-boat obviously wasn't turning back up the Elbe to Hamburg. But mostly they were sensations of utter confusion. Confusion that he must not permit to show on his face, or in his words. Obviously he was supposed to be fully acquainted with the mystery at the Hamburg basin. *Magnet* planes, the German had said? A submarine was made to go *under* water and not *over* it?

The questions shot through Combat's brain and his whole body seemed to become charged with electricity as a tiny inkling of an idea took form, it was impossible, too utterly fantastic even to give it further thought. Yet he couldn't stop thinking about it. Submarines traveling over water? *Over water?* Could that be what the dead Agent 16 hadn't had time to tell Brainbridge? That U-boats were being flown from their shore bases *over* the British naval blockade? It seemed incredible, yet....

The U-boat commander speaking again cut short his thoughts.

"*Ja.* I will enjoy slipping through under their swine ships," the man said. "That's the way we did it in the last war, and that's the sailor's way, anyway. You airmen can have the planes as far as I'm concerned."

"It is the airplane that will win this war, I think," Combat said with a shrug. "Take tonight. Supposing an enemy squadron had come over to bomb the basin? What then?"

"*Himmel!*" the other snorted. "What would we submarine men care? We would only dive and get away from their bombs. But those cursed magnet planes? They are fast, yes, and two of them can carry a submarine to ten thousand feet. But once they are landed on the water they are helpless. They would be blown to bits, and everything else along with them. Mark my words! Once our enemies discover our little secret at Hamburg the magnet planes will have to find another base. Aircraft? The curse of the *Vaterland*. Aircraft, aircraft! Everything must be in the air. Bah, I say! I do not like it at all."

The German finished with a loud snort, glared for a moment at Combat, and then poured himself another drink. He downed it in two long gulps and slapped the empty glass back on the wall table.

"*Ja*, curse the damn planes!" he snarled anew. "They are taking our right to fight away from us. This cruise we're on, now. Torpedoes we carry in our hold? Yes, but not for us. For the aircraft. We will be nothing but cargo boats before the war is over. *Gott*, the hours I have dreamed of the moment I would give the command to fire at an enemy ship crossing my sights. But, now? *Bah*, we set the torpedoes afloat, then sneak away and let the damn airmen get all the glory. It is too bad the Leader was not born a sailor. He would then realize how we are being humiliated by your fool air comrades."

Once again the commander ran out of breath. He started to pour himself another drink but thought better of it. He leaned back against the wall, jammed his big hands deep in his sea jacket pockets and sat glaring at the opposite wall. Instinctively Combat refrained from looking at him; forced himself to stare down at the deck so that the German might not see into his eyes and guess the confusion in his brain.

And a turmoil of confusion it was, too. What the German had said was echoing and reechoing in Combat's head. He knew now that his crazy, almost insane surmise actually was the truth. Magnet planes! The German had said that two magnet planes could carry a submarine clear up to an altitude of ten thousand feet. So that was the way the Nazis planned to defeat England's blockade? To fly their U-boats to their patrol areas in the North Atlantic. It seemed almost unbelievable... yet, God, it *must* be true!

"What matters is winning the war," he said quietly to get the German talking again. "Not just how we do it. Seamen, airmen, or soldiers, we are all Germans, *Herr* commander. How long shall we be on the cruise? We lay torpedoes, you say? I do not think I understand that."

The quick sharp look the U-boat commander suddenly flung at him caused Combat to hold his breath in fear he stuck his foot into it.

"If you don't understand, then you probably haven't been told," the German snapped. "But the longer this cruise lasts, the happier you should be. They are not pleased with you back in Hamburg. Only now I found out over the radio the damage that was really done. You have cost Germany five brand new submarines, my airman friend!"

COMBAT WANTED to go into a cheer over that bit of news, but naturally he refrained. He forced a stunned, puzzled look to his face.

"Five submarines, *Herr* commander?" he gasped. "But how? The explosion when... as you say, the magnet planes broke contact?"

"Partly," the other growled. "The five U-boats had been flown down to deep water from where they were constructed inside Germany. They were on the surface as you yourself must have seen. All the hatches were open, and the conning towers. For inspection. The explosion caused all five to take water. They foundered and sank. True, they can be raised, but it will take many days. They even dragged one of the magnet planes down under, too. The electron cups, I believe they are called, could not be cast off in time. No, my friend, your *Kommandant* is not pleased with you at all. You are lucky we must continue on our way to make the test, instead of turning around and taking you back to Hamburg. *Bah!* Our nice little torpedoes for the airman. It is enough to make brave sailors weep with shame!"

"The test you sail out to make has to do with torpedoes?" Combat asked and held his breath.

"But of course!" the German barked. "The navy high command wishes to make sure the Athenia was no mistake. So we go out into the shipping lanes to lay the torpedoes for more tests. *Mein Gott,* they make my beautiful little boat a guinea pig for you men who fly! We might just as well remain tied up to our docks. It is...."

The commander stopped short as there came a knock on the door and the officer of the watch stuck his head inside.

"The breakwater is sighted *Herr* commander," the junior officer said. "Your orders were to inform you."

"Naturally," the senior one growled. "Who else on this boat could take us through the mine fields? Did I not plot them, and superintend their laying, myself?"

"Yes, *Herr* Commander," the other said meekly. And waited for orders.

"Then get topside!" the commander roared. "I shall be up presently."

The junior officer ducked out and the commander looked at Combat. A hard smile tugged at one corner of his mouth.

"Your superior thinks a little work would be good for you, *Lieutenant,*" he said slyly. "And you know the respect I hold for airmen, by now, don't you? Well, first we'll see what kind of a sailor you are. Put on that sea coat and come topside on the conning bridge with me. The wind and spray is nice off the breakwater. I'll show you what navigation really is. Hurry up; I can't wait here all night."

Combat nodded and immediately started to climb into the heavy sea coat slung over a chair on the other side of the room. He would have given a lot just to be allowed to lie down and rest his aching bones. But he knew there was small chance of that. The spite a certain U-boat commander had for airmen was going to be taken out on one Lieutenant Schmidt of the German Air Force. And that man, Schmidt... was a Yank!

The icy blast that hit Combat the instant he stepped, out onto the conning tower bridge with the U-boat commander chilled him straight to the core. With an effort, he curbed the shivers that raced through him because he was conscious of the commander watching him out of the corner of his eye. To hell with giving the German any opportunity for gloating satisfaction.

A moment or so later, though, the Yank was too busy with his own thoughts to care whether or not the German was pleased. Brain spinning over at top speed, he tried to classify all the information he had gained since leaving Posen. But when he was all through he was still pretty much in the dark. However, two things he knew definitely. What the dead Agent Sixteen had said was true. The Germans were flying their submarines over the British blockade by something they called magnet planes. And from what the U-boat commander had said about the sub being little more than a mine cargo boat. Combat supposed the Germans were sinking ships by radio torpedoes. Guiding torpedoes to their mark from the air! The sinking of the Athenia had been but a test? He wondered if any of the survivors had reported they'd seen a plane in the air. Probably not. The craft could fly high, perhaps even above the clouds and guide the death-dealing missile to its mark.

"And now I'm to see them make another test?" he breathed to himself softly. "See another helpless, unarmed passenger ship go plunging down? Not if I can help it, by God!"

But even as he half whispered the last, he laughed bitterly within himself. Fat chance he'd have of stopping them, once the deadly torpedoes had been cast afloat. And speaking of his chances in anything, a hell of a fine lot of headway he was making. Pinneberg been his goal, and now he was more or less a prisoner aboard a U-boat heading out into the wave whipped North Sea to dive under the British Fleet and continue on into Allied shipping lanes. Perhaps they'd be gone a day, or a week, or a month. Then, too, perhaps they'd be gone forever. The Allies were certainly on the watch for Hitler's steel fish, just as they had been in the last war. If by a rotten break they should be sighted… it might be curtains.

His utter helplessness and inability to take command of the situation irked Combat like a knife twisting in his heart. He knew so damn little, and questions that might gain him further information might end up in his unknowingly giving himself away. Heinrich Staube! The one man who might be able to clear up the double mystery was still just a name to him. With every revolution of the sub's screws his chances of ever finding the man were growing less and less.

COMBAT GRITTED his teeth in savage desperation and stared out across the black water of the North Sea as the commander skillfully guided the sub through the mine booms and out into the open sea. For the moment, he bitterly regretted having given his promise to Lord Brainbridge to find Heinrich Staube. Better that he had returned straight to England and the Air Force. If he had done that he might this very moment be on patrol, instead of doing what he was doing… taking a ride on a German U-boat, against his own wishes.

"Cut it!" he breathed to himself. "You've got your life still, haven't you? You've found out a little that's important, haven't you? Isn't that something? Damn right! So keep your head, you sap, and watch for the breaks!"

The pep talk he gave himself helped a little, but not for very long. Gripping remorse stole over him again. Even the telling to himself over and over again that he'd put five U-boats and one magnet plane out of commission for a while, failed to raise his spirits. Out of sheer desperation to keep his thoughts off his temporary setback, he tried to plot ways and means of smashing the tests the U-boat would make. However he didn't get very far with that, for apart from knowing that the boat was going to release floating torpedoes he was not any too sure just what the nature of the tests would be. A ship was to be sunk, though. Yeah, and if he could spend just ten seconds or so in the wireless room, he....

"The *swine*, to come in this close! All hands below! Sound the signal for a crash dive! Her light will pick us up in another minute!"

The orders that roared from the commander's lips jerked Combat out of his unhappy reverie. Then a hand smashed against the small of his back and he was almost sent headlong down the conning tower ladder.

"Lively, you dundering airman!" the commander roared. "Do we stand here and let them shoot us out of the water?"

Combat had seen nothing in the darkness, but as he started scrambling down the conning ladder he did catch the flash from the roving beam of a ship's searchlight a mile or so off the starboard bow. And from what the commander said he knew that some Allied patrol boat had slipped in close to shore. If that swinging searchlight picked up the U-boat, hell would be popping in no time.

As though the gods were waiting for that bit of stark truth to flash through Combat's mind, the opening of the conning tower hatch above him suddenly became bathed in brilliant white light. The patrol boat had spotted them! The searchlight beam did not move onward. It stayed put and in a couple of seconds there came the faint boom of a gun. Then the air above the U-boat was filled with whining sound. The whine changed into a dull roar that made the U-boat quiver from stem to stern. And then Combat received the commander's boot between his shoulders and he fell sprawling down the last few rungs of the conning tower ladder.

"Slow dog!" the German roared and leaped over him to the control board.

Combat picked himself up as the conning tower hatch clanged down into places. Bells and sirens sounded from one end of the U-boat to the other. The high hum of the electric Diesels shoving out the diving planes cut through all other sounds. Made enough to take a swing at the iron-faced commander at the control board Combat curbed his wrath and glanced about. The U-boat was on her way down, and it seemed that every pair of eyes in the control room was riveted to the depth gauge. The needle swung down to ten feet, to twenty, thirty, forty, and fifty. Past fifty it went, then down and down. Combat had the crazy sensation that the boat was hurtling straight to the bottom, like a lifeless thing of steel. His head hammered and he could feel his eyes bulge in their sockets. But he remained standing, with his eyes, too, glued to the depth gauge.

At two hundred feet the commander raised one hand and shouted an order without taking his slate grey eyes off the board.

"Trim ship!" he roared. "Hold her steady. Check fore and aft tanks. Stop motors. Detector stations!"

Sailors went scurrying past Combat. In spite of his hatred for their breed, he was forced to admire the efficiency with which they carried out their individual tasks. There was no wasted effort. In a matter of seconds the commander had his reports from every part of the ship. The U-boat hung motionless now in the water like a steel coated whale, asleep. Every man seemed to have stopped breathing. The needle of the depth gauge hung at the two hundred foot mark, as though it were painted on the glass. The commander had fixed his eyes on a junior officer seated at the propeller detector gear. The young German twisted knobs and closed his eyes as though in doing so he might the sooner pick up the sound of the surface ship in his earphones. A tense moment passed.

Presently he turned his head and looked at the commander.

"Almost directly above us, sir," he said. "A few degrees to port perhaps."

The commander simply nodded. He said nothing, but Combat felt a sudden chill as the cold slate grey eyes swiveled around to bore into his own. Then suddenly a sound akin to an express train rushing headlong into a giant boiler came from above. The U-boat trembled, seemed to heel over a bit, and the half dozen emergency lights winked rapidly. But they remained on. Then another boom of sound shook the sub more than the first. Every face seemed to turn a little green in the pale light. The muscles of the commander's face twitched with hate. He half turned his head toward the officer at the detector. That man nodded slowly and a smile parted his thin lips.

"Going away, sir," he said. "They dropped a couple for luck, I guess. She's going away fast, sir."

"We'll wait just the same," the commander growled. And once more his eyes swung around to meet Combats. "We were lucky this time," he grated through clenched teeth. "You, airman, get forward and report to Lieutenant Kragg. Perhaps we'll hold our luck if we put our jinx to work!"

CHAPTER 13
SATAN LAUGHS

I T WAS daylight and a fairly warm sun bathed the rolling swells of the North Sea. Once again Bill Combat stood on the conning tower of the U-17 with its commander. The undersea craft was making lazy headway and members of her crew were busy opening hatches fore and aft. It was difficult for Combat to keep his eyes, open, because he was dog-tired and dead for the want of sleep. And he was inwardly boiling with cold rage at the slate-eyed, hatchet-faced German who stood at his side. Over twelve hours had passed since a British patrol boat had tried to blast them out of the water with depth charges. And every minute of those long hours had been a nightmare to Combat. A nightmare because he had become more and more convinced that the submarine's commander was a madman.

The German's actions had proved it beyond all doubt. He was a man possessed with two fanatical ideas. One was discipline aboard his ship. And the other was savage hatred for the German Air Force. Hatred for those he swore were robbing him of his rightful chance to do service to the Fatherland. His moods changed like a swinging pendulum. One minute he would put Combat to the dirtiest task on the boat, whatever it happened to be at the time. And then roar at the Yank that it was nothing compared to the punishment he'd receive when they returned to Hamburg.

Then suddenly he would relieve the Yank of the job, take him to the officers' wardroom, feed him a drink, and force him to be an audience of one to all the injustices inflicted upon one Commander Cramer. That off his chest, the German would suddenly go into reverse. He would discuss war problems with Combat, treat him as an equal in rank and be most friendly. Then out of a clear sky the man would fly into another rage, and order the Yank back to work.

It took all of Combat's willpower to keep his hands off the man's neck. But he did refrain from that little thing because common sense told him he'd gain nothing. Mad or sane, Commander Cramer was a skilled U-boat commander, and although his officers and crew feared him more than a little, Combat could tell they had a high respect for his ability. And another reason Combat took it all on the chin with no outward complaint was because he was adding to his knowledge of the secret of the German radio torpedo. Cramer knew a lot about it, obviously, and every now and then, when in one of his friendly moods, he would let slip a bit of information that Combat would file away in his brain for future reference.

However, the main reason the Yank held himself in was because of the realization of his own helplessness. Half a dozen times he had tried to reach the radio room unobserved and flash a warning to British boats of the U-17's position. Its position he was able to keep track of from hour to hour, but as far as sending it out over the air, he didn't have a chance.

And so, once again, he stood on the bridge with Commander Cramer. When the hatch covers were off the crew started hauling long black cigar objects up out of the hold. They were torpedoes. Combat recognized them at once. However, they were considerably different from all others he had ever seen. To begin with there seemed to be no war head on the nose. It was fairly blunt and had a small plane on either side, like the diving fins on a submarine. Half way back on the top, a small brass rod stuck straight up some three feet or more, and two strands of copper wire went from the tip of the rod to both the fore and aft sections of the missile. The tail of the torpedo came back to a sharp point, and the screw was set underneath at an angle, and fitted in the middle of a small diamond-shaped rudder.

The crew hoisted half a dozen of the doom-dealing weapons to the deck, and then, under the supervision of a deck officer, lowered them over the side and cast them loose. Combat watched through agate eyes, and grimly weighed the sense of trying to stop the work. But even as he thought of it, he knew how useless any attempt would be. Whether he liked it or not, he could only watch and wait for the best break. And, for the time being, the only break would be a chance to get to the radio room. But the helpless inactivity galled him. In twenty-four hours he hadn't accomplished enough to cover the head of a pin. He....

"There!" Commander Cramer's growl broke through his thought. "We're rid of the things. Now it's up to your wonderful airmen. And before I'll believe anything I've got to see it with my own eyes. There, see? They have sunk to a hundred feet where they'll stay until the radio plane pilot decides to use them."

"A hundred feet?" Combat echoed. "So a ship won't hit them? But I thought you said that contact won't explode them. They can only be set off by radio."

"A precautionary measure until they are really proved," the other grunted. "I don't like the things, though. Might ram one of them, myself, and foul the propeller. Radio mines, that's what they are. And I say, rubbish! A real torpedo, shot from a tube, *that's* the thing! Yes, marksmanship. There's sport in killing the swine that way. But this? Thousands of feet up, guiding the damn thing by radio? *Bah! Gott,* I have two real torpedoes aboard. If I sight something, I'll blow it out of the water and be damned to you airmen. *Himmel,* would I like to sight another *Athenia!* Wouldn't even give the swine a look at the periscope! I'd blow them all to hell and—"

The madman stopped abruptly as the radio officer came up the bridge and saluted smartly. "Well?" the commander roared when the other just stood there holding a yellow sheet of paper in his hand.

The radio officer cast a quick glance at Combat, then instantly returned his respectful gaze to the senior officer's face.

"Just received this from Hamburg, sir," he said. "It was coded, urgent, so I had it decoded at once. Here, sir." He passed the message to his commander.

THE COMMANDER snatched the yellow sheet from his hand, bent his head and read it. Watching him, Combat saw the German's jaw muscles tightened; saw the piglike eyes narrow to slits, and then the ghost of a tight smile tug at one corner of the mouth. The senior officer stuck the paper in the pocket of his sea coat and waved his other hand.

"Return to your post!" he snapped. "I'll take care of this."

The radio man saluted again and ducked down into the submarine. A cold chill rippled over Combat's heart as the German commander turned toward him and smiled... an oily smile.

"That was about you, *Lieutenant* Schmidt," he said slowly. "You are Schmidt, aren't you, eh?"

Alarm bells sounded in Combat's brain. He was conscious of the German's right hand slipping into the pocket of his sea coat.

"But of course," Combat said in a puzzled voice. "Why do you ask?"

"There were perhaps two Schmidts in your Hamburg squadron, eh?" purred the German. "And you were perhaps mad at each other last night? A little affair of honor, perhaps, settled by machine guns over the Hamburg Basin? Was that it *Lieutenant* Schmidt?" the officer asked.

Combat's heart was pounding against his ribs. He didn't need three guesses to realize that the German was toying with him as a cat toys with a mouse. It meant in plain language that they had found out at Hamburg that the real Lieutenant Schmidt had died. Therefore, he was naturally the unknown pilot who had been attacked. Inwardly Combat cursed himself for ever letting himself be hauled aboard the U-boat. He realized now that at the time he had been but a couple of miles from shore. He might have made it... but, of course, he hadn't known *then*.

"You are making a little joke, *Herr* Commander?" he asked

with a forced grin, and kept one eye on the German's hand concealed in his pocket.

"A joke, yes," the other nodded and roared with laughter. "But the joke is on you. Just now I have received word from Hamburg. Well, the sea often gives back its dead. It did this time. The body of *Lieutenant* Schmidt has been recovered… and identified, naturally. And so, they are wondering at Hamburg who *you* are. And you must be most important, yes. Do you know who sent this radio?"

"My *Kommandant*, no doubt," Combat said with a nonchalant shrug.

"Perhaps," the U-boat commander said, and also shrugged. "Is your *Kommandant*, *Herr* Hermann Peiplow, chief of Nazi Intelligence?"

Combat gasped in spite of himself, and for a crazy moment he was afraid his knees were going to buckle under him. They had suddenly become as gobs of limp rubber. Hermann Peiplow, chief of Nazi Intelligence? The very thought of the name sent Combat's mind racing backward in memory. Way back to the Imperial Hotel in Berlin. Nazi Intelligence… the Gestapo! The plot to kill his mother and him. The escape from Germany and his mother's death. Brainbridge saying that the Nazis must have taken him for Agent Sixteen. The third attempt on his life that had resulted in Brainbridge's death. And now a radiogram from Peiplow in Hamburg.

The Yank groaned inwardly. He was caught like a rat in a trap. He knew something else the radio contained. Orders to Commander Cramer to place him under close arrest and return him to Hamburg. No, he didn't know it, exactly, but he could make a good guess. He knew beyond all doubt that the German navyman's hand in his pocket clutched a Luger. One false move and the madman would be delighted to pull the trigger. His only hope… if such could be called a hope… was to stall for time.

"No, he is not my *Kommandant,*" he said with a frown. "I do not understand. What is this all about, anyway?"

"You will find out soon enough," the other said and laughed. "Meantime you are my prisoner. The orders read for you to be returned to Hamburg on the radio plane. Yes, I think perhaps I shall miss you… *Lieutenant* Schmidt!"

Combat closed his eyes for the flickering of a second. God in Heaven, he had waited twelve hours for this? Floated around on this cursed U-boat only to be slapped in irons and flown back to Hamburg… for God knew what? He had waited, wasted time, and then, like a blundering fool, thrown all hope for success to the four winds. So near, yet so very, very far. The torturing thoughts whipped around in his brain and stabbed him to his very soul. Then something seemed to snap in his head, and wild, insane recklessness took charge of him. At least, by God, he could do *something.* He'd get to that radio room and warn the British of as much as he could. By God, yes….

"You do not feel happy, no?" the German's leering voice came to his ears.

Combat steeled himself, looked sheepish and lowered his head. "No," he mumbled.

The U-boat commander started to laugh but he didn't finish it. No sooner had the man opened his big mouth than Combat flew into furious action that caught the German flat-footed. A smashing right to the jaw rocked the German back on his heels. At practically the same instant, Combat lashed out with the other hand and spun the man around and pinned his gun hand. Then up came the Yank's crashing fist again in a beautiful hook under the jaw. Every ounce of his one hundred and ninety one pounds was behind the blow. The U-boat commander seemed to raise straight up in the air. He hit the bridge railing with the small of his back. Momentum carried him over backwards like a fancy diver. He hit the lower deck on his head, glanced over its curving side and went splashing down into the water.

Combat didn't wait to see the man take the dive. The instant his blow landed he leaped toward the conning tower ladder and went down it like a flash. Half a dozen racing steps aft took him to the wireless room. The officer on duty gaped as he burst in through the door. And that's all the radio man did. Combat knocked him sprawling to the floor, out stiff as an iced fish. Slamming the wireless room door, Combat rammed a chair under the knob and then leaped for the panel board. A flick of the switch set the sending generator to humming. He waited precious seconds for it to warm up and then jerked his hand to the key.

Body tensed, heart hammering against his ribs, he sent his SOS out over the ether waves. He gave the sub's position, reported that radio torpedoes had been dropped, and directed British scouting planes to drive all enemy craft from the shipping lanes in that area, at all costs. Over and over again he repeated the message, praying in his heart that it would be received. He wanted to pause and throw the receiver switch to check an answering call, but he didn't have time. All hell was breaking loose beyond the jammed door. Fists were pounding against it and voices shouting hoarsely. Above the roar he heard the saw-toothed snarl of Commander Cramer. The man had obviously been fished aboard by those on the aft deck of the submarine. Too damn bad!

The blue flame crackling across the spark gap every time Combat pressed the key, the Yank hammered away for dear life. Then suddenly the door gave way with a crash. A corner of it clipped him on the shoulder as it fell inward. The impact knocked his hand off the key and sent him spinning to the floor. In a flash he was on his feet. He lashed out one fist and had the savage satisfaction of knowing it smacked the U-boat commander's purple face. Again he struck, but his blow went wide. In the next half second a dozen German seamen roared into the room. The Yank fought furiously, savagely, but the odds were too great. The U-boat seemed suddenly to fall down on top of his head and he went floating off in a sea of silent darkness.

CHAPTER 14
HELL ON HIGH

THE LOW muttering sound seemed to come from a thousand miles away—from way out beyond the rim of the world of shimmering shadows in which Bill Combat suddenly found himself. His brain, as though awaking from the sleep of the dead, tried desperately to grasp the meaning of the sounds that penetrated his ears; to trap them and make some sense out of them. But for a long time the sound simply droned on and on, while the shimmering shadows drifted back and forth across the mirror of his brain.

Eventually though, the shadows started to clear up a bit; to more or less take definite shapes and form, while the muttering drone became more and more distinct. Suddenly, his brain grasped the meaning of it all. The muttering sounds were words being spoken in German. No sooner had he realized this than the curtain of memory parted in his head. And then, like blinding light slashing the darkness, he knew he lay slumped down on the floor of a cabin plane in flight, and that not ten feet from him were two men speaking German to each other.

He stared at them blankly for a few moments. One wore the uniform of a Nazi flying captain. The other wore civilian clothes, and as Combat stared at him a cold chill trickled down the small of his back. The civilian was standing sideways, but even in profile that face portrayed all the heartless ruthlessness and cunning it was possible to find in one human being. The man was old, his hair was a dirty white and the musty-looking skin was drawn tight over the jaw and cheek bones. The eyes were mere slits under the almost hairless brows. If ever Combat had seen a brother of Satan, he was seeing one now.

Tearing his gaze from the ugly profile, Combat looked past the two Germans at the object of their attention. At first glance he thought he was looking at a miniature sized motion picture screen. It was a square yard of milky glass screen, hung on the forward wall of the compartment. To its left was a small door that Combat knew instantly must lead to the pilots' compartment of the plane up forward. He dismissed that realization, even as it came to him, and then returned his attention to the screen.

Milky waves, like sea swells, were rippling across the screen. At the top was a five inch oval shaped blur. At the bottom was another oval shaped blur only it was no more than an inch in length. In between were six little red dots, all in line. And as Combat peered at them he saw them move about between the two oval blurs like soldiers on drill parade. And then he suddenly realized that the ugly looking German was making the red dots move about by means of a little knob he moved over the surface of a flat black disc fitted to the wall at the right of the screen. When the knob was moved to the right, the dots wheeled in line and moved in that direction. If the knob was moved upward, toward the large shadow, the dots followed. In short the dots could be moved in any direction desired.

Fascinated, he watched. Then the German flying captain grunted in obvious admiration, and spoke.

"It is almost like magic, *Herr* Doctor Wolfgang!" he cried. "*Gott*, I can hardly believe it possible. The Leader will make you an honored man in Germany if you are successful."

"*If* I am?" the ugly one echoed in a voice that was half way between a croak and a hiss. "Already I have been successful. It was one of my radio torpedoes controlled by my beloved Blau Wave that sank that swine English boat, the *Athenia*. And from this very plane, too."

The words were like shafts of lightning striking Combat's

brain. He was on the radio plane Commander Cramer had spoken about? Hell yes, he remembered, now. He was to be flown back to Hamburg on the radio plane. Such had been Hermann Peiplow's orders. Yeah! And so obviously he had not been killed when Cramer's men had swarmed into the radio room. Why? Peiplow's orders had been *a la* Frank Buck? To bring him back alive? Again why?

Doctor Wolfgang was speaking again. Combat shoved the thoughts into the back of his brain.

"I do not worry about success," the man said. "I have not made use of Heinrich Staube's brain for nothing. His ideas were crude, but I have perfected them. When I have finished I'll get rid of the swine. *Gott*, what a fool he's been over his woman!"

"I do not understand," the other German said with a frown. "Who is this Heinrich Staube, *Herr* Doctor?"

"A fool with the brain of six men," the other snapped. "It was he who discovered the Blau Wave, and this radio torpedo. He also discovered this Red-Ray lens that can produce on a screen what lays below the clouds. What you are looking at now. That British boat there at the top and Commander Cramer's submarine there at the bottom. And the Blau Wave brings out those little red dots that are the torpedoes Cramer put into the water not an hour ago. Yes, he discovered all that while working for me in my laboratory."

The satanic looking German paused to throw back his head and laugh. Laughter that made Combat think of a cat yowling in the middle of the night.

"The fool became frightened when he realized what wonderful weapons he had discovered for Germany," the man continued after a while. "He wanted to destroy them; to kill himself. But I fixed that. His wife was a *schweinehund* Jewess, and he loved her so very much, *ja!* I convinced him that if he did not continue his work; did not obey my every order that his wife would be punished as only Jews can be punished. *Gott,* he groveled at my feet like the dog he really is. He swore eternal allegiance to me if I would see that his swine wife was spared. I agreed."

"No Jewess deserves to live!" the German flying officer growled.

"Of course not," the other grunted. "So she died in the concentration camp, naturally. Only the fool, Staube, does not know it. He thinks the letters he receives each week are from her. But he won't be receiving many more. *Gott,* no!"

BLIND RAGE surged through Combat. The blood hammered at his temples, and impulsively he started to lurch up onto his feet. And it was then he realized for the first time that his hands were lashed behind his back. Instinct caused him to relax and close his eyes. But his brain did not relax. It was tortured by thoughts of the bitter truth. Like a thousand white hot needles piercing his brain cells.

One by one the shafts of blinding truth stabbed him. First, his radio efforts aboard the submarine had been a failure. For some reason he would probably never know, his frantic SOS appeals to patrolling British ships had not gone out over the ether waves. That was certain because Wolfgang's words told him that the radio plane was cruising about over the spot where the submarine was. The submarine and an unsuspecting Brit-

His fist jammed the words
in the Nazi's throat!

ish ship, low down on the horizon and out of sight. Of course, Cramer had said that radio torpedo tests were to be made on the first enemy ship sighted in the lanes. And there was the picture on that yard square screen right before Combat's eyes. The British ship, the red dots that were the submerged torpedoes and

Cramer's boat that was undoubtedly down to periscope depth. And up here, high in the clouds, a son of Satan was explaining his death dealing toy and playing with it until it suited his fancy to send those little red dots streaking for that large oval blur at the top of the screen.

No, his SOS messages had not gone out, otherwise there would not be that scene below. He was a helpless prisoner. At any moment Wolfgang might tire marching those red dots around the screen. At any moment they might blast English lives into all eternity. If the test failed, Cramer's boat was there to make sure. Death hanging on a single thread of time. He was helpless—hogtied and on his way to be turned over to the whims of Hermann Peiplow, the most feared man in the Third Reich.

Clamping down hard on his jangled nerves Combat tried to twist his hands this way and that in order to loosen the cords that dug painfully into his skin. Seconds perhaps, before death struck. Dear God, please help him! Please let him loose before that offspring of Satan sent those red dots swinging toward the top of the screen.

"Yes, I will be finished with that dog, Staube, very soon," more words came from the mad doctor's lips. "This test today will not fail. As official observer for the Leader you shall see for yourself, *Herr Hauptmann.* If you like, your hand will send the torpedoes to that English ship. You simply guide this knob I now touch, and when the red dots are by the shadow that represents the English ship, you pull down this switch. That creates the current that will explode the torpedoes and blow the boat out of the water. Right now I have all six of the torpedoes under single control. However, with the Blau Wave, I can direct one at a time, if I wish. I can leave five below the waves for another day, and just use one. But this time we will use them all. There will be nothing left of the British ship, and the swine aboard her will never know what happened."

"*Himmel,* this will be sport!" the other German breathed. "Why, we will even be able to radio-guide your torpedoes up the Thames to London and blow up the ships right at the docks. Here, let me work the control guide knob, *Herr* Doctor."

As the flying officer reached for the knob, moved it over the surface of the black disc, and made the six little red dots wheel this way and that, sweat poured down off Combat's forehead. Sweat caused by heartfelt dread for human lives soon to be sacrificed to the gods of war. And sweat caused by the savage straining of his wrists against the cords that held him fast. But he gritted his teeth against the pain, closed his eyes to slits and remained on the alert to instantly go limp should either of the Germans turn around. He struggled desperately with the cords.

They dug deeper and deeper into his flesh. He could actually feel skin being scraped off, and the warm trickle of released blood. But he didn't stop for an instant. The German flying officer was like an insane child. He pushed the guiding knob all over the disc and made the line of little red dots fairly dance. A half dozen times Combat's heart leaped up to clog his throat as the line of dots swept toward the shadow of the British steamer only to be checked in the nick of time and sent wheeling around in the opposite direction.

Presently the German seemed to tire of the fun. He let go of the knob and looked at his ugly companion.

"Did this Staube also discover the electromagnet power used on the Magnet Planes?" he asked.

The other shook his head vigorously.

"No," he declared. "That is my little secret and mine alone. It is right here in my head, and shall remain there forever. I am not a fool, my friend. I am not like Staube. My usefulness to the Reich shall never come to an end. Ah yes, there are one or two close to the Leader who do not like it that I stand so high in his favor. They would like to purge me, *ja*. But so long as the secret of the Magnet planes is in my head, they do not dare. And so I am quite comfortable, yes indeed."

The mad doctor paused and chuckled gleefully.

"And my biggest surprise is soon to come, my friend," he said presently. "Within forty-eight hours I shall accomplish a task that will stun the world and make me the most honored man in all the Reich. Ah, yes, I shall perhaps be as worshipped as the Leader, himself."

"I would take care of how my tongue wagged, if I were you, *Herr* Doctor," the flying officer said. "Not even Goering would say words such as that to another's ears!"

Combat saw the red flush through the ugly face. Saw the sharp needle pointed teeth as they were bared in a grimace of contempt.

"And you will do well to watch your tongue, my friend!" the doctor snapped. "It would not go so well with you if I should report you attempted to interfere with my test, today. Perhaps you forget that most of the money for this equipment you see before you came from the Leader's purse. True, you observe for him. But you would be a fool to waste his money for him, eh?"

The flying officer cursed sharply in annoyance, then made an angry gesture with his hands.

"Enough of this!" he grated. "You have explained all that I need know for the moment. Let us get on with the tests and see if they are successful. Some swine English patrol boat may blunder into sight."

"So much the better," the doctor snorted. "But very well. All is ready. Take the guiding knob and place your other hand on the explosion switch, there. When the red dots...."

The mad inventor's voice droned on, but Combat didn't listen. Guns were roaring in his head. Guns exploding with his mighty efforts to yank, and pry, and drag, and haul his hands free. The pain was almost unbearable and for minutes he had kept his teeth clamped down hard on his lower lip to keep back any groans. Then suddenly, when there seemed not an ounce of strength left in his arms, one of the cords gave a little.

THAT FACT flooded him with hope; redoubled his efforts. He got one thumb free, then the forefinger, then the middle finger... and then his whole hand was free. Both hands were free! For a split second he battled with himself; fought savagely to drive the weakness and weariness from his body. And then he stopped all that sort of thing. The German flying officer's hand was on the knob and the line of six red dots were moving toward the shadow at the top of the glass screen. For one crazy instant Combat thought he saw the hand gripping the detonating switch whitening at the knuckles.

From a slumped position on the cabin floor he virtually hurled his body upright. Even as he came to his feet the German doctor whirled around. Gleaming hate blazed in the slitted eyes. The twisted mouth opened and hideous sounding cries poured forth.

"The prisoner! He has escaped! He is free! He...."

Combat's sledgehammer fist drove the rest down the yawning red throat, and the small Luger clutched in the doctor's hands fell to the floor of the cabin. Without so much as changing step, Combat hurled the goggled eyed doctor to one side by mere contact of his charging body, and went sailing onward toward the other German. The flying officer kicked out with his foot and tried to jam the guiding knob way up to the top of the disc. But Combat had left the cabin floor in a wild flying tackle that carried him clear over the German's upraised foot.

One hundred and ninety-one pounds of American bone and muscle hit that German pilot square amidships. There was a sound like a blast furnace door suddenly being opened, and then the German let go of the guiding knob and the exploding switch and fell over backwards like ten tons of brick. Combat landed on the man hard, then scrambled to his feet, reached out and grabbed the guiding knob.

"Down this way, pals!" he grated and wheeled the little red dots toward the smaller shadow that was the U-17.

The dots moved toward that shadow with maddening slowness. Combat cursed them to greater speed. Out the corner of his eye he could see the blank-faced German pilot struggling slowly to his feet. Holding the knob way down at the bottom of the disc Combat waited for the red dots to follow. At the same time he kicked out backwards with one foot.

"Stay put, lug!" he grated.

His aim was bad, however. At any rate it was the German's turn to dodge a kicking foot, and he did. In the next split second strong arms were swept about Combat's body, and an attempt was made to hurl him across the cabin. His hands, gripping the exploding switch, and ready to throw it the instant the red dots reached the small shadow, was torn loose. Without wasting effort to try and grab hold of the switch again, he suddenly let himself go limp in the German pilot's embrace. Then, just as suddenly, he straightened up fast and snapped his head back. It was as though an axe had been whanged down on top of his skull. He was faint and dizzy from the sharp pain. But his heart leaped as the arms entwined about him, pinning him practically helpless, dropped away. He caught the German flush under the jaw with the top of his head and knocked him forty ways from Sunday.

Panting and gasping for breath, Combat swung around and forced his dancing eyes to focus on the glass screen. The line of red dots were right up against the small shadow. Out shot his hand. He grabbed the detoning switch on the right and threw it into the contact grooves. As though by magic the line of red dots winked out. The small shadow danced around on the screen for a second, and then changed into a great black bulge that grew bigger and bigger. The U-17 was no more!

And then a Luger cracked, and a finger of white pain was

drawn across the back of Combat's neck. He ducked and spun around in the same movement. The mad doctor was on the floor on one knee. His face was a twisted mass of devilish hate, and a thread of smoke was curling up from the muzzle of the Luger in his hand. For the millionth part of a second Combat looked straight into the mouth of certain death, and then the unbeliev-able took place off to his left. A second Luger cracked, and the gun went flying from the doctor's hands to slap against the far wall and drop down onto the cabin floor.

"You fool, Wolfgang! *Herr* Peiplow's orders were to deliver him alive. And that shall be done!"

Combat turned his head to look at the German pilot. The man was bleeding at the mouth, and a couple of his teeth were missing. He was back against the wall, and his gun and his eyes were both fixed on Combat. Words slurred off his dripping lips.

"On the floor with your hands behind you, dog!" he hissed. "This time I shall tie the knots. And do not thank me for saving your dirty life. I will be delighted to kill you later… in my own way. But first one will obey orders."

Combat shook his head and grinned as he slowly sank to the floor and lay on his face with hands behind him.

"Twice they try to wash me out," he muttered. "And twice they save my hide. This Peiplow must be screwy as hell. Or maybe the guy just can't make up his mind. And, Combat, old sock, here's hoping like hell on that last crack!"

CHAPTER 15
NAZI CUNNING

HERR DOCTOR WOLFGANG'S radio plane came down to a landing on one of the several military airports about Hamburg with all the swiftness and certainty of a mechanical bird sliding down a tight wire. No sooner had the wheels been braked to a stop than a squad of German troops, led by an officer, raced out and completely surrounded the craft. In the radio cabin Bill Combat stared bleakly at the opposite wall, seeming not to care what happened next. Inwardly though, he was on fire with torturing thoughts. The fact that he had failed stung him to the core. True, he had met with a little success. Two hours ago he had added the U-17 to the ever growing list of submarines that would no longer do the Third Reich any good.

That had been but a minor success—no more than a tiny drop in the bucket. One Heinrich Staube was still as much of a mystery as ever. No, not quite that. From Wolfgang's lips he had heard much about the man. But what he had learned only served to thicken the mystery about Staube. What connection did Staube have with the dead Agent Sixteen? For what reason had Sixteen pleaded with Brainbridge to contact Staube. Thinking it over, Combat could make a pretty good guess at that, but there was no way to prove that his guess was correct.

Yes, he'd met with a couple of minor successes to be sure. He knew how the Germans planned to beat the British blockade with their magnet planes that could carry submarines far out to sea; to take them places in a few hours that would take days under the craft's own power. And, yes, he knew about the radio torpedoes. He had actually worked the machine, himself. But what did all that get him in the final analysis? Nothing! Not a damn thing, because he was heading toward certain doom. In Hamburg, Herman Peiplow awaited him. The chief of Nazi Intelligence had finally caught up with him. True, it was a bit surprising that the Nazi had ordered him to be brought back alive. Yet he thought he could guess the answer to that. Undoubtedly Peiplow still believed that Combat had been working in Germany as one of Brainbridge's agents, and the German was going to make sure.

That thought made faint hope beat in Combat's heart. There was still a chance for him to play cards in the dangerous game of war and death. If he could keep Peiplow guessing, the longer he would be allowed to remain alive. And the longer he remained alive, the better his chances of smashing the Nazi attempts to fight England with radio torpedoes and magnet planes. And then, too, Wolfgang had said that his greatest triumph was still to come... *to come within forty-eight hours!* Combat wondered what that could be, and little icy chills started rippling up and down the small of his back.

And then he stopped wondering. The ship was on the ground and the door of the radio compartment had been flung open. A German staff major stuck his bullet-shaped head inside, gave the flying officer and Wolfgang a quick glance and then fastened his black eyes on Combat.

"So you are the swine, eh?" he growled, *"Ja,* I remember seeing you at the aircraft factories about Berlin. Well, your little store of information will probably die with you, *ja*. I will take charge of the prisoner. You two will report to Herr Peiplow at once. And I would not care to be in your shoes, *Herr* Doctor Wolfgang!"

As the major spoke the last to the two Germans in the compartment he made a motion with his hand over his shoulder. Then he stepped aside and two beefy soldiers appeared in the doorway. They laid hands on Combat as though he were no more than a sack of meal and lifted him bodily out of the plane. Still holding him off the ground they carried him over to a waiting car, dumped him in the rear seat, and climbed in beside him. The jolt caused the bullet crease in Combat's neck to burn, and white dots began to swim around before his eyes. He closed his eyes for a moment and clenched his teeth hard. Little by little the pain and dizziness passed. He opened his eyes again, just in time to see the major push his fat hulk behind the wheel. Gears meshed and the car shot forward like an arrow leaving the bowstring.

Bracing himself as best he could, and trying to prevent all his weight from resting on his securely bound hands, Combat turned his head and looked around. The car was leaving the flying field and sliding up grade toward the outskirts of Hamburg in the distance. To his right he could make out the many canals that intersect the eastern and lower parts of the city. And he could also see the Alster River which becomes the Binnenalster and the Aussenalster when it reaches Hamburg. The spires of St. Nicholas and St. Peter's churches looked like golden swords pointed toward Heaven in the sun. But what caught the eye first, and maddening to the German natives of Hamburg, no doubt, were the lofty spires of the magnificent Jewish temple. It stood out like a cluster of sparkling diamonds against a black velvet background.

To all of that Combat gave but a glance, however. What finally caught his attention and held it was Hamburg harbor. The submarine and magnet plane basin, to be exact. That lay off to his left and ahead, and as he stared wide-eyed at the huge jet black pterodactyl shaped wings resting on the water, he found it hard to believe he wasn't really seeing an aeronautical mirage. The strange ships looked like gigantic bats from another world. The engines were streamlined into the leading edge of the thick wing, and the pilots' cockpit was a rounded glass hump in the very center of the leading edge, at the point where the wing retreat, or sweepback, starts on either side.

A FEW of the engines were ticking over, but obviously they were simply being tested. The craft were securely moored, and not pointing out to sea or into the wind. Then suddenly Combat saw the one on the far side of the basin. One half of its giant wing was under water, while the other half pointed up toward the sky. A glance told him that it was the magnet plane the real Lieutenant Schmidt had crashed into the night before. He peered at it intently, and because of the tilted position of the plane, he could see the thick cable that came out from underneath the wing. Half way along its length it forked, and at the end of each of the forks was a large vacuum cup some twelve to fifteen feet in diameter. These were undoubtedly the electro-magnetic cups the U-17's commander had spoken about, and for several seconds Combat stared at them fascinated.

Then his attention was turned to the other end of the basin, and what he saw brought a grim smile of satisfaction to his lips. There, diving boats and crews were striving to raise five water-filled submarines to the surface—the same five U-boats that had foundered when the magnet plane had exploded.

"Too damn bad it didn't sink them all," Combat grunted.

For words spoken aloud he received a fist in his aching side, and the guard who did it snarled through his teeth.

"Silence, swine dog!"

Combat grimly steeled himself to the increased ache and returned his gaze to the basin. It did him no good, however. At that moment the car reached the top of the rise of ground and turned off in the other direction, and the basin passed from Combat's sight. Then followed a ten minute ride through the outskirts of the city. The news of Combat's capture had evidently been given out, because civilians and soldiers alike lined the sidewalks of the streets through which the car passed. They jeered and hurled curses at him, and Combat could not help but feel grateful that the major at the wheel didn't stop the car and order the two guards to hurl him out to the mercy of those Nazi wolves.

Finally the car was braked to a halt before the entrance of a three-story gray-stone building. At a nod from the major the two guards hauled Combat out of the car and into the building. There they walked him down a long hall to a door at the far end. While one of them opened it, the other released Combat's bound hands. Then, with a grunt, the German booted Combat in the small of his back. Unable to keep his balance the Yank went flying into the room, where he tripped and fell sprawling on his face. The door clanged shut behind him.

For a moment he lay where he had fallen, gasping for breath. Then slowly he picked himself up and stood erect. A glance around told him he might just as well have stayed where he was. There wasn't a single piece of furniture in the room. Nothing but a ceiling, a floor, and four walls. There were cracks at the top of the walls to allow for circulation, and, as Combat looked at them, he wondered if, by chance, there was a dictograph beyond. Obviously the room was some sort of a prison, and likely the entire building was a jail. Thus, when two prisoners were stuck in the room, their conversation, if any, could be overheard.

"Well, I haven't started talking to myself, yet," Combat grinned to himself. "And they'll just waste time waiting."

The wait-cure, however, seemed to be Combat's fate. The minutes dragged by into an hour, and nothing but silence came to the room. Not even the ghost of a sound from beyond the four blank walls. The hour became two hours, three, four, and five. Combat's nerves became like bunches of tiny fire-crackers exploding in all parts of his body. He tried pacing the room, but that didn't help at all. And when the sixth hour of silence dragged to an end, it was all he could do to stop from hammering his fists on the door and screaming at the top of his voice. Anything to end the soul-gripping silence.

To add to his tortures, the pangs of hunger began to tie his stomach into knots. And he would almost have been willing to sell his soul for one drink of clear cool water. If the torture was kept up much longer he was afraid he would go nuts. But the thought of leering Nazi faces gave him the strength to keep a grip on himself, and to force himself to wait, and wait… and wait.

FINALLY THE waiting did come to an end. The door was unlocked, opened, and his two guards came inside. Without a word they took him by the arms and lead him outside and up a flight of stairs. At the top they knocked upon a door, waited for the summons from within, then entered. The room in which Combat found himself looked very much like an American courtroom. There was a judge's bench, a jury box, and chairs and tables for lawyers and their staffs. There was even a witness chair, and into this chair the guards hurled Combat.

Blinking back the pain, he looked up at the man seated on the bench, straight into the snake-green eyes of Hermann Peiplow, chief of Nazi Intelligence. Once, in Berlin, he had seen the man on the street, and anyone who had once seen Peiplow would never fail to recognize him the next time. Combat stared at the man for a moment, and then let his gaze travel about the room. There were ten or more others present. He saw Wolfgang, the radio plane pilot, the bull necked major, two or three other officers, and a civilian. The civilian was an old man, whose thin hair was white and stringy, his eyes a watery blue, with the skin of his face like faded parchment stuck to the bones. Yet, when the man's eyes turned suddenly toward Combat, the Yank had an impression of white flames flickering in their depths.

And then Combat had no more time for an inspection of the room, or of its Nazi-branded contents. Hermann Peiplow was addressing him.

"You seem to possess a charmed life, *Herr* Combat," the German said with a smile. "I almost find myself feeling sorry you did not reach England."

Combat grinned and jumped at the opening the words gave him. "Who said I was trying to *reach England?*" he asked disarmingly.

He was instantly rewarded. Peiplow frowned and cast a quick glance about the room. Combat noticed that the German's eyes rested on the old civilian much longer than they did on anybody else.

"So you were not trying to reach England?" Peiplow echoed after a while. "Perhaps hoping to contact Lord Brainbridge's Agent Sixteen, eh?"

"Perhaps," Combat nodded. "You haven't seen him around, have you? I was under the impression that for once your bum marksmen didn't miss."

The German scowled darkly, opened his mouth to speak but seemed to think better of it.

"I don't believe you realize your position, *Herr* Combat," he finally said in a quiet voice. "The fact that you are an American citizen is not going to help you much, you know. By your acts of the past few days you have openly committed yourself to bow before England's king."

"One man worth bowing to," Combat said. "I'm all for him. He's doing a swell job. So what?"

"So under the law we have a perfect right to shoot you for a spy in England's employ!" the other said harshly. "However, it is in my power to change your punishment to imprisonment until after the war. It's entirely up to you."

"Well, what do you want to know?" Combat asked suddenly.

Every face in the room lighted up in stunned amazement. Even Peiplow's jaw dropped a bit. He leaned forward and stared down hard at Combat.

"You admit to be one of Brainbridge's agents, eh?" the German murmured. "I knew I was right from the start. Well, *Herr* Combat, there is much you can tell me, if you wish to save yourself from being shot. An Agent, now dead, stole some valuable papers. It is believed he turned them over to Lord Brainbridge, along with other information he had. You were close to Brainbridge, of course. A few days ago you met him in Posen. He gave you instructions. Probably told you who to contact next, and so forth. Well, *Herr* Combat, what instructions did Brainbridge give you?"

Combat looked at the man and realized perfectly well that Peiplow did not expect a truthful answer. He had a feeling the German was leading up to something else.

"You don't expect me to tell do you?" Combat grunted.

The other smiled, evidently very pleased in the belief he had trapped his prisoner into an important admission.

"So you did receive instructions, eh?" Peiplow echoed. "Well, you can tell me later. I have various ways of making people talk. Right now, look at the old man, there, with the white hair. Do you know him? Have you ever met him before?"

Conscious that every eye had suddenly become riveted on his face, Combat looked at the old civilian. And what he saw caused him to start inwardly. Fear such as he had never seen in a human face before leaped into the other's eyes. Stark fear and pleading that came from the very depths of the soul.

"No, to both questions," he finally said. "Why?"

Hermann Peiplow didn't answer him. The German even stopped looking at him and stared at the old civilian instead.

"I will believe for the present that the prisoner speaks the truth, Heinrich Staube," Peiplow said. "But I am still not sure you didn't help the English. You may go, now, but remain close. Perhaps I may have another letter from your wife for you... or perhaps something else. Get out!"

The old fellow mumbled something, and then twisted the cap he held in his hands and started shuffling toward the door. Combat had the sudden wild insane desire to laugh out loud. Of all the cockeyed twisted turn of events! There, not a dozen steps from him, was the one man in all Europe he wanted to meet. Heinrich Staube! And damned if Peiplow hadn't asked him if *he* knew Staube. The desire to laugh swept on past and in its place came an urge to run after Staube... to yell to the man that the Nazi rats lied. To yell that his wife was dead, and that they no longer could hold that threat over his aged head.

But the old fellow went out the door, and Combat's attention was jerked back to Peiplow. The German was staring at him again and talking.

"Do you wish to tell me what Brainbridge found out from Agent Sixteen, *Herr* Combat? Or shall we wait until later?"

The Yank drew a deep breath, looked the German straight in the eyes and played his cards for time... for delay.

126

"I never talk on an empty stomach," he said. "Maybe a little food and drink would refresh my memory."

Peiplow laughed. "You expect a lot for a swine spy," he said. "Food and drink, eh? Well, we shall see about that, my foolish friend. Take the prisoner to Camp Twenty. Perhaps he will like it there."

As Peiplow spoke the last to the bull-necked major, memory tingled in Combat's brain and an icy chill stole through his body. Camp Twenty! He had heard of that famous Nazi prison in the dim past... scraps of the truth picked up here and there. A prison? Far from that! It was a place of Nazi torture. There the beasts of Berlin buried their enemies, political and otherwise. And buried is the word. It was vowed on all sides that no man had ever returned from Camp Twenty alive. There they were tortured and punished beyond mere words of description. There they died.

Combat did not have to guess his immediate fate. Peiplow and his entourage of killers would have their "fun" as long as it lasted. And then... and then, at least, merciful death.

CHAPTER 16
DEADMAN'S PRISON

B ILL COMBAT sat on the cold stone bench in his musty, vermin-ridden cell at Camp Twenty, just staring at the opposite wall. He supposed he had been there for three or four hours, though he had more or less lost track of time. In a dull, abstract sort of way he knew that daylight had passed, and that night had come again to Europe. He had only to turn his head and look out the small barred window of his cell to prove that. But he didn't bother to turn his head. What difference did it make whether it was night or high noon? He was locked up in the famous Nazi prison of torture. And if he still did not believe it to be true, he had only to listen to the sounds that came from the other cells. Moans and groans of pain; the harsh curses of Nazi jailers; the savage crack of a whip, or the thump of a club, and the wailing cry of the doomed that followed. And echoing it all, the hoarse laughter of the guards.

Thus far no one had come to his cell, but he was not particularly surprised at that. Nazi methods were no secret to him. They first weakened their prisoner both mentally and physically by giving him the silence and hunger cure. In that way it was much easier to smash his resistance with the whip or club and get him to tell that which they wished to know.

"Maybe I was wrong," he muttered in a low broken voice. "Maybe I shouldn't have given the rats the idea I knew plenty. Yet, hell… my only hope was to stall for time. Yeah, to stall for *this!*"

Fists clenched helplessly, he got to his feet and moved to the narrow window. All was black outside, but even in daylight he would only have seen a section of the vast lowlands about Hamburg. But he didn't go over to the window to look, but to hear. To hear a sound… sounds that made his heart turn over in his breast, and tears of raging helplessness to sting the back of his eyeballs. Close by in the darkness was a flying field. He could hear the purr of engines being warmed up. And every now and then the mighty, full-throated roar of some craft thundering into the air, away on its mission of war and blood and death!

God in Heaven! They might be radio planes heading out to sea. They might even be the Magnet planes taking U-boats far out into the Atlantic ship lanes. Yes, they might even be planes roaring away to create the mysterious triumph of which Doctor Wolfgang had spoken. And there he was, trapped between musty cold stone walls. Trapped between the jaws of Nazi death with perhaps the next hour to be his last.

Almost unconsciously he lifted his two fists and beat them on the stone window ledge.

"If I'd only got some word through!" he moaned. "But I didn't... I didn't. And they don't know a thing about those radio torpedoes, or the Magnet planes. Oh God, how I have failed!"

The pictures of what might be happening outside because of his failure to get word through to the British rose up in his brain to taunt him. Try as he did to beat them back, to brush them aside, they simply returned in force, more taunting and soul twisting than ever. And for the glimmer of a second his brain, body, and nerves threatened to fly off in all directions like a released bunch of springs. But with a mighty effort he slammed down hard on his jittery nerves, and cursed himself back to sanity.

"Damned if I'll give them the satisfaction of seeing me go batty!" he grated. "I'll...."

He clipped off the last and stood frozen by the window with every one of his senses on the alert. After a moment he heard it again. It was a faint brushing sound. Something like a twig or a small branch being drawn across stone. And then, in a flash, he realized what it was. Just outside his prison cell were shrubs. Somebody was moving slowly through them. Moving slowly toward his window.

As soon as he was positive the sound was moving his way he went back a step from the window, dropped into a half crouch and waited, fists bunched. Perhaps it was his turn now to suffer at Nazi hands. Perhaps this was the first move in their little game of human torture. He didn't know, and there was no way of telling. But, yes or no, whatever it was he wasn't going to take it lying down. Not by a damn sight, not so long as he had two fists and life left in his body.

Five seconds that seemed as five years dragged by, and then the sound stopped. Stopped directly beneath his cell window. Hardly daring to breath, he waited, eyes fixed on the window opening. The opening was little more than a blur that blended in with the rest of the darkness about him. Then suddenly he saw movement. A shadow, darker than the rest oozed up over the window sill. And then came the whisper, so faint, that for a fleet split-second he wondered if it was his imagination playing tricks with the rest of his brain. The whisper came again:

"*Herr* Combat!"

Impulsively he moved close to the window; put his face against the bars.

"Yes?" he breathed. "Who are you?"

"Not so loud!" came the soft hiss through the bars. "I am the old man, Heinrich Staube. I must talk with you. I have got to talk with you. Did you know one Lord Brainbridge? Tell me, please!"

The mighty Breman began
rising out of the sea!

131

"He was my uncle," Combat whispered. "I have been hunting for you, Staube. You've got to help me get word to the British. The Hamburg Basin must be destroyed. They must be warned to clear the air of radio planes. Without the planes, the radio torpedoes are useless. They...."

"Be quiet!" the other purred. "All the walls have ears in Germany. I am helpless. I cannot help you. I love England, yes, but I would not dare lift a finger against the Nazis. I must work; must give them my brains. *Gott*, if only I *could* die! For two long years that Wolfgang has made me his servant. My brain is his servant. *Himmil*, you will never know all the things my brain has discovered for the swine. And I dare not stop. But tell me... did you know a man who served Lord Brainbridge? He was known as Agent Sixteen. Is it true that he died? I have heard rumors."

"Yes, Agent Sixteen is dead, Staube," Combat whispered. "He died in my uncle's arms. And his last words were for my uncle to find you. I saw my uncle killed, and...."

"His last words were to find *me?*" the other cut in breathlessly. "Yes, yes? What did he say? What was the message to give me?"

"Message?" Combat echoed with a frown. Then as a sudden thought came to him. "You knew Agent Sixteen well, Staube?" he asked. "It was you who stole those papers; who told him of the radio planes, and the magnet ships?"

"Yes, yes," the other said hurriedly. "I told him a little to prove my faith in him. He was my wife's brother. My darling Lena. And in return he was to find Lena for me. To visit her and then come and tell me all about her. Here they read my letters from her. She would not dare to say if she is unhappy. *Gott*, my poor,

poor Lena! Why did the dear God ever give me this brain for the Nazis to use? They laugh at me, and torture me, and I dare not but obey. To the others I am just a poor ship's carpenter. A little crazy, yes. But all the time I am really the brain of that dog, Wolfgang. I invent things to kill people with. And I have to do it or they will kill my darling Lena. Ah, dear *Gott!* I must live so that my Lena will live."

A dry sob stopped the old man for a moment, but before Combat could say anything, Staube was speaking again.

"What did Agent Sixteen say?" he begged. "Tell me, what was his message from Lena? You must know! Tell me, and... and maybe I will try to help you a little. But I must know my Lena is safe, and happy, and that she still loves me as I love her. *I must know!*"

COMBAT COULD almost feel the old man trembling as he clutched hold of the cell window bars. The Yank started to speak, but suddenly he was afraid to tell the old fellow the truth. The truth might result in God knows what. The man might go crazy. His marvelous brain might crack and he would go jabbering and jabbering away leaving Combat still imprisoned and worse off than before. No, as low a trick as it might be, he must first get Staube to help him escape from the place before he told him the bitter truth. God, he felt like a worm even to think of offering that kind of a reward. However, he was forced to steel himself against the pangs of his own conscience. Staube was but one man; an old man who would be happier dead, now. And out there in the war, on land, on sea, and in the air, were brave men ready to offer their lives that Hitler and his beasts of

Berlin might be wiped from the face of the earth. Their lives were worth the saving. And after all, Heinrich Staube would want to die when he learned of how he had been tricked into giving all of his brain for the love and safety of one who no longer lived.

"There was a message," Combat whispered slowly, then gritting his teeth. "I will tell you when you help me escape from here. You can do it, Staube. I *know* you can do it!"

Combat held his breath when he finished. And then he slowly let it out when Staube's words told him he had scored a direct hit in the dark.

"Yes, I can help you escape," the old man said. "They let me come and go around here because they think I am harmless. Besides I have a small laboratory on the top floor where I work sometimes. And *Gott*, if you did escape you might warn the British. So long as the Nazis do not harm Lena, it is nothing to me if they fail. And *Gott*, I would like to see that dog, Wolfgang, fail this night."

The fires of hope and excitement leaped high in Combat. He reached out both hands and gripped Staube's clutching the bars.

"Warn about what?" he demanded. "What is planned for tonight?"

"Much," the other said. "Today a squadron of radio torpedo planes have been fitted up for action. Tomorrow morning they will fly out and destroy the entire British North Sea Fleet. Before dawn, thirty U-boats will have been flown over the blockade and set down in the water. They will put their load of torpedoes over the side, *in back of the blockade*. When daylight comes the radio planes will take the air. The British will never know what happened. Torpedoes will crash into them from the rear. No periscopes about. Nothing. The radio planes will be above the clouds. The British ships will go down like rocks."

"So that is Wolfgang's triumph, eh?" Combat breathed more to himself. "To wipe out the British blockade over night?"

"No," Staube whispered. "That is but part of it. The radio planes, and the Blau Wave are from my brain. His secret is the electro-magnetic power by which his Magnet planes can lift great weights and fly them far out to sea. And tonight he attempts something that will stun the whole world. Something that even to me, a scientist, seems almost impossible. However, I believe it will be done. Wolfgang's electromagnetic current is the most powerful thing on the face of the earth. It…."

"What is he going to do?"

"The steamship Bremen," Staube said. "Three days ago it sailed from New York. The British could not find her. Wolfgang received the news only this morning. She is hiding close to Iceland awaiting orders to proceed to Russia. But the Leader, himself, has given Wolfgang permission. *Gott*, if he succeeds and I believe he will, yes!, it will be as a miracle turned into fact. Already six of his Magnet planes have left."

"Magnet planes?" Combat gasped. "Good God, you mean…?"

"Within a few hours Wolfgang will attempt to lift the Bremen from the water and fly her over the British blockade and set her down in the Elbe here at Hamburg. But enough of that. I will help you escape if you tell me the message from Lena. What was it?"

Combat fought with himself for a moment or so. He wanted

to reach through the bars and try to comfort the old man as he told him the heart-breaking truth. But thoughts of what the Nazis planned for the night killed the urge. The entire North Sea blockade fleet sent to the bottom? Forgive him, dear God, but to prevent that, if he possibly could, was worth far more than the lives of a hundred old men.

"When I escape I will tell you, Staube," he said, hating himself with every word. "It is a message you should hear… but I will not speak it until you have got me out of this place. Now, will you do it?"

There was a long moment of silence punctuated by a soft sob from the old man.

"Very well, I will," he whispered. "Go over and wait by the door. You will hear me turn the key. Count ten, then open the door and go to your right. There is a short flight of stairs at the end. Go half way down them and wait. I will meet you there and lead you the rest of the way. I'm leaving, now. Ah, my darling Lena, when will we be together again? I love…."

The old man's voice was lost in the darkness as he moved away from outside the window. For a second or so Combat stood staring out into the darkness. Then, as the revving of airplane engines penetrated his ears again, he breathed a fervent prayer of wild hope and slowly crossed the musty stone floor to the door.

CHAPTER 17
PURPLE PERIL

ACTUALLY, THE turning of the key in the door lock made little more noise than a feather being brushed across black velvet, but to Bill Combat's straining ears the sound was akin to that of a gun explosion. His first reaction was to reach out and grasp the curved iron handle and yank open the door. But he curbed the urge, grimly forced himself to count ten slowly. Then he did grasp the handle, twisted and pulled the door open a crack. He looked out into a stone hallway filled with shadowy pale light. Moans and groans of the suffering prisoners came to him louder, now. But every door he could see was tightly closed.

He took a precious second or so to steel himself, then slipped out the door, closed it behind him and went down the hallway, hugging the near wall. He found the flight of stairs at the end leading down. It was dark below, and as he oozed down, he had the wild crazy sensation of going down into a bottomless black pit. When he reached the first landing, he paused. Almost instantly a hand reached out from nowhere and gripped his. His heart zoomed up to smack against his back teeth, and it was all he could do to refrain from wrenching his hand free and lashing out with both fists. After all it was not beyond the realm of possibility that Staube's visit to his cell window had been but a trick by Peiplow to trap him into attempting to escape. It is much more sport to shoot the panther in full flight than to shoot him in his cage! But Staube's whispered words dispelled that fanciful idea, and he swallowed his heart back into place. He stood there tense.

"Do not speak!" came the warning. "Follow me and step carefully."

During the next thirty seconds Combat might have been led through the very heart of darkest Africa as regards any idea of direction. He was led upstairs and downstairs, through corridors, and through doors. Half a dozen times Staube pressed them both back into black shadowy recesses where they waited, heart in mouth, while the sound of footsteps or voices in the distance faded away.

And then suddenly the old man led him through the last door and Combat felt the cool night air on his face. But Staube did not stop there. Hugging the blackness of some heavy undergrowth, Staube continued on until they were hidden in the fringe of some nearby woods. Beyond the woods came the sound of flying activity, and through the leafless branches, Combat could see the glow from take-off and landing lights. Then off to his left came the sudden and mighty roar of super-powerful engines. He guessed what they were, even as Staube gasped aloud.

"*Gott*, the Magnet planes!" the old man breathed hoarsely. "They are already starting to fly the U-boats out to sea. You must hurry if you are to reach the fleet and warn them in time, *Herr* Combat. Perhaps you can steal a plane from the woods. You wear a Nazi uniform, you know."

The suggestion was already a concrete thought in Combat's brain. He nodded, and then suddenly gripped Staube as a question he had asked himself several times in the last two days came to his brain.

"The Magnet planes," he said speaking rapidly, "is it possible to hear them on the radio... when they are in the air, I mean?"

"Only if you are at their level," the old man said. "Their radios broadcast a signal that travels ahead. Thus, any German craft in the air at that altitude will be warned of the armada's approach and the pilot can get out of the way. The first time newly built submarines were flown from the inland factories, down to the testing basin here at Hamburg, four German planes on patrol were rammed and sent to earth. The special steel wing of one of those radio planes could almost cut a passenger transport in two, and not even feel it. Get out of the way if you hear their signal when you escape. But, now, I have done my part. Give me my message. I must hurry back in case they look for me. What did my darling Lena tell Agent Sixteen?"

Combat suppressed a groan of misery for the old man. The moment had come, and he was almost tempted to turn and race away, leaving Staube still ignorant of the heart-chilling truth. But he had given his word to the old fellow. And after all, Staube did deserve to know the truth. Dammit, he should be told. It was only right, and fair.

"Get a good hold on yourself, Staube," Combat said gently and laid a hand on the other's arm. "There really wasn't any message. The dirty rats have been lying to you since the beginning. Your poor wife didn't even write those letters you've been receiving. I first heard it from my uncle. And I also heard Wolfgang tell one of the pilots of the radio plane that brought me back to Hamburg. Staube, your wife died in a Nazi concentration camp. I'm sorry—from the very bottom of my heart. But… but try and think of it this way. Your wife is happy now. Far more happy than she could have been alive in this rotten world. Those Nazi butchers killed my own mother, so I know how you feel, friend. I…."

The last was drowned out by a night slashing scream of wild anguish that poured from between Heinrich Staube's parted lips. Impulsively Combat put out his other hand to calm the man, but Staube spun around and went racing away. His heart-freezing cries seemed to rise above the revving of aircraft engines, beyond the wood—to fill the night with sound.

"Lena is dead! They lied to me! She is dead. They killed her… killed her… killed her! God curse their black hearts! They killed her… killed her… killed…."

The sounds were choked off into silence as the old fellow probably tripped and fell sprawling in the bushes. Combat shuddered in spite of himself, and then glanced up toward the cloud filled heavens.

"Go with him, God," he whispered. "Go with him, God!"

As the last word left his lips, Combat wheeled and plunged into the woods. Zigzagging around bushes and tree trunks he headed toward the edge on the far side. When he reached it he sank panting down behind a bush and peered out at the scene. Some twenty-five to thirty craft were lined up on the tarmac and most of the props were ticking over. His heart leaped with high hope, and for one insane second he wanted to let go with a war whoop of joy. It was as though Lady Luck, herself, had been saving this moment for him.

THE FIELD before him was obviously the home drome of Wolfgang's radio planes. There they were all in line with mechanics swarming all over them, making ready for the great flight shortly after dawn. In addition to the radio ships there were several smaller craft, single-seaters and interceptor ships, which were obviously going to serve as escort planes to decoy and harass the British fleet while the radio ships did their deadly damage.

For a moment or so Combat stared longingly at the radio ships, but presently, he squashed the hope. With all those mechanics swarming over them he wouldn't stand a hope in hell of making off with one of them. There wasn't a chance. Besides, you couldn't pilot one of those babies and work its trick gadgets at the same time. The pilot and radio compartments were separate.

Nope! The radio ships were out. His best bet was to....

He cut off the rest and grinned. At that moment his eyes had come to rest on a German Dornier light scouting bomber, not sixty yards from where he crouched. Its prop was ticking over, a mechanic stood slouched against one wing... and all six of the hundred pound projectiles of devastating doom were fitted in the racks underneath the thick, stubby monoplane wing. Hells bells! Lady Luck was not only smiling upon him, she was laughing out loud.

"That puts you in the slot, guy!" he whispered excitedly. "Get moving!"

141

Absently straightening his somewhat rumpled Nazi uniform, he moved out from behind the bushes and walked, not too fast and not too slowly toward the mechanic slumped lazily against the wing-tip. Finally the greaseball saw him and stiffened instantly to attention. Combat gave him the hard eye and stepped close.

"The pilot for this plane!" he demanded in harsh German. "Where is he?"

The mechanic pointed a slightly trembling finger toward the far end of the tarmac.

"He has gone for his maps and flying orders, *Herr Lieutenant,*" he said.

Combat made an impatient gesture with one hand.

"The *dummköpf!*" he growled. "Go and summon him here at once. I have his orders! Hurry!"

The mechanic gulped, nodded, saluted, and got his feet in motion. Combat waited until he was three or four planes down the line then leaped quickly into the cockpit. In one continuous movement of his hand he released the wheel brakes and jabbed the throttle forward. The powerful Benz in the nose roared up like a startled, angry lion, and the craft fairly leaped forward. His body braced, Combat took the shock, opened the throttle wider and lifted the ship clear. At five hundred he flattened out, banked back toward the field and stared down. A hundred or more white faces were turned up toward him, but nobody was moving. His sudden take-off had seemingly created an epidemic of Nazi paralysis.

Combat grinned, wheeled about at the far end of the field and started down in a flat, but lightning-like dive.

"Catch, rats!" he bellowed. "I can only spare you a couple!"

As he spoke the words he reached for the bomb release toggles and sent one load of destruction hurtling earthward. It struck the third plane in the line, let go with a howl of hell, and spewed white, yellow and orange flame out in all directions. Leveled off, Combat streaked down the line and let the second bomb go. No sooner had he yanked the toggle than he sticked the nose heavenward. The terrific concussion seemed to reach up and press against his wings and speed him on his way. When he finally stared, down over the side it was as though the earth had cracked open and permitted him a look straight into Satan's mansion. The line of planes was now but a wide ribbon of licking and crackling flame, out of which grotesque figures ran, or crawled, or dragged themselves away. Just two bombs and there weren't more than three of the thirty or more ships left untouched, if that many.

"The rats make sweet bombs," Combat grunted wheeling away. "I'll hand them that much. Now for the next job on the list. Stay with me Lady Luck!"

COMPLETELY FORGETTING the destruction he left behind, Combat wheeled around toward the Hamburg basin, hunched forward over the stick and peered ahead. The basin twinkled with many lights, and then suddenly, powerful floodlights were turned on and night about Hamburg became as bright as high noon. Magnet planes and U-boats leaped up into Combat's vision in clear relief. Two Magnet ships, their secret electromagnetic cups clamped fast to the fore and aft sections of a U-boat, were slowly moving across the surface of the water. The first section of the night air armada was about to take off!

"Think so?" Combat roared and slammed down in a howling dive. "Not if I can help it, rats!"

Prop-wash screaming past his half-opened glass cockpit cowling, Combat dived straight for the nearest Magnet plane. Without taking his eyes off it he reached out his free hand and made sure his twin-firing Spandaus guns were loaded and set for action. And the instant he made sure he whipped down his hand and jabbed the electric trips. The guns streamlined into the nose, and the leading edge of the wing yammered and chattered their hail of hissing death downward. But Combat saw his bullets smack against those powerful wings below, then bounce off like so much rice thrown against a window. Bullets, against those gigantic things of the air, were just a waste of time.

Cursing he zoomed up and circled around for another dive. And as he did so all hell came spewing up toward him. Archie batteries, on the edge of the basin, had started their savage attempt to blast him clear out of the sky. And out the corner of his eye he saw half a dozen patrol planes streaking up into the air.

He gave all that but a passing glance. The Magnet planes had the U-boat clear of the water now and were slowly lumbering upward, higher and higher, and gaining speed with every rev of their propellers. For a split second, the weird, fantastic sight held Combat in its eerie grip. Then he cursed, shook himself free and howled downward again. Down, down he roared, straight through the blasting archie fire, until it seemed he was going to smash straight into the huge wings. But the last split second he flattened out, yanked back the bomb release toggle twice and sent two packages of hell on their way.

The instant they were released he zoomed upward, twisted his head and looked down. It was almost as though the gods of war had held off these bombs until he had turned his head. For at that moment he saw both of them slam down through the pilots' compartment in the very center of the wing.

"Bullseye, and with bombs, by God!" he thundered. "So that's the spot to hit, is it—?"

All hell was touched off in that second and its very fury rammed the last of his words back down his throat. A mighty volcano of splashing fire leaped up from the nose of one Magnet plane. Then, as the huge craft careened on a wing, a sheet of brilliant purple spewed from the submarine's side. Combat had just enough time to see both Magnet planes and the flaming submarine fall back into the water. Then he had leveled off and was streaking clear of the red and purple flames that leaped as though to set the overcast heavens afire.

"Strike one!" he roared. "And here we come again!"

Wheeling about when he was a mile or so from the basin, he started down again in a wild power-dive. The patrol planes were in the air by now and their pilots tried desperately to cut in front of him and blast him to hell and gone. But those Nazi butchers might just as well have tried to reach out and stop a bolt of lightning with their bare hands. Combat simply ignored them and howled down toward the Hamburg basin that was now becoming little more than a basin of red, yellow, and purple flame with each new tongue of flame heralded by a thunderous explosion.

Traveling at top speed he winged straight through the spewing flame and smoke and sent the last of his bombs hurtling earthward. Then banking, he headed northwest toward the mouth of the Elbe and the North Sea beyond. That is, he started to bank around, but he cut the maneuver short as a bit of hellish drama down below caught his eye. He saw a man running along one of the U-boat docks that stuck out into the basin.

An old man with thin grey hair flying in the wind. It was Heinrich Staube gone stark, raving insane. One glance told Combat that, as he switched his gaze to the head of the dock, to the fast cabin seaplane moored there, he saw the ugly figure of *Herr* Doctor Wolfgang.

In the middle of that roaring and flaming hell Staube had finally found his betrayer, and now he raced toward him, barehanded and unarmed! Impulsively Combat yelled a warning, but his voice was lost in the roar of his own engine. Then he saw jetting flame spit out from Wolfgang's hand and from the hands of two or three Germans about to board the seaplane with him. Staube staggered and reeled on the dock. He clutched both hands to his stomach and kept on running.

Again and again the guns barked at him, but though bullets pounded and hammered into Staube's body, the old man still came onward. Then, when his outstretched hands were but a few feet from Wolfgang's throat, Staube tottered for the last time. He fell forward on his face, tried to get up but lost his balance, then rolled off the edge of the dock into the water. Even in death the gods had cheated old Heinrich Staube.

"I'll even it up for you, old fellow!" Combat bellowed and started straight down through that licking hell. "I'll...."

The yammer of Spandaus guns off to his right cut short the rest. The patrol planes had caught up with him at last. And out of the corner of his eye, he saw Wolfgang leap into the swift seaplane; saw the craft streak off down a strip of water still untouched by the purple hell, and finally lose itself in the smoke.

"Heading out to meet the Bremen, of course!" Combat yelled and automatically kicked out from under one of the diving patrol planes. "It's not too late, Staube! I'll even up for you, yet!"

But as Combat finished the last, his eyes happened to fall on the radio panel in his cockpit. It was as though the gods had decided it was his turn to be kicked in the face. A burst of shots from the patrol planes had smashed into the cowling and smashed the radio into a pile of twisted junk. One look told him it wasn't even worth the trouble to see if the thing was functioning. Fate was having the last laugh, it seemed. Flying death was hemming him in on all sides, and he was utterly helpless to inform the British that the Bremen, the pride of German's merchant marine, was up there off Iceland. Perhaps even now it was clear of the water and being flown southward to safety. And Wolfgang, the murderously mad inventor, was on his way out to meet her and to escort her home in triumph.

CHAPTER 18
SATAN'S FINISH

THE VERY thought of the Nazi vulture caused something to snap in Combat's brain. A wild howl burst from his lips and in the next second he became a thing of crazy, reckless fury, darting and twisting and gun-spitting about the flame-tinted skies about Hamburg's Elbe River. In as many minutes, two patrol planes went hurtling earthward to destruction, their pilots probably never knowing what hit them until they woke up in the Devil's parlor.

However, their loss served only to add to the savagery of those left in the air. They hurled their craft at Combat from all directions. But they were not fighting any ordinary pilot that night. They were up against a steel-clawed eagle who felt neither fear nor pain nor anything save white rage. A mechanical comet he became and nothing between heaven and hell could stop him. Three more of Hitler's pretty boys went down in flames, and then, with a vicious maneuver that virtually made the Dornier squeal in protest, Combat ducked away from the rest and went tearing up into the clouds and safety.

No sooner was he in their billowy security than he snapped on the instrument dash light, held his breath and took a look. Lady Luck was still with him. Only the radio panel had been knocked haywire. The rest of the instruments, particularly the compass, bank indicator, and blind flying horizon, were unharmed.

"Praise be to their lousy marksmanship for that," he murmured, and banked the ship.

As soon as he was on a compass course for Iceland's waters, he relaxed a bit in the seat, and made sure that his guns were reloaded and in working condition. Then he set himself firmly for the flight ahead. Seconds passed into minutes, and the minutes added up into hours. When his calculations told him he must be out over the rolling waters of the North Sea, he slid down from the clouds to make sure.

His calculations were correct. A limitless expanse of uninviting water stretched out beneath him. He could just make it out in the poor light. And as he unconsciously glanced toward the east he saw the first thin line of a new dawn. A bitter truth assailed him then. The radio! Not only was he unable to send word to the British fleet and send them hell-bent after the Bremen, but he was equally unable to tune in for the Magnet armada's signals. In other words he had to find the armada with his own eyes. And a glance down, at the water was all that was necessary to tell him that his vision would soon be blotted out by the rolling fog now sweeping from the north.

Where was the Bremen, now? At what time were the Magnet planes supposed to contact her? Was the Bremen in the air, now, or was the great ship still in the water? These and countless other questions tore through his brain as he thundered forward. Several times he thought he spotted British patrol boats down through the fog. But he did not dare go down to make sure. First, because it would take time and he'd have to crash-land on the water and wait to be fished out. Secondly, because those shapes he saw below might be German patrol craft.

But the thing that really made him roar onward was his

strong belief that he was close to Iceland's waters. The minutes had totaled hours now, and if he'd figured the Dornier's speed correctly, he should be close to the meeting place with the Bremen.

"Unless she's already in the air, and has actually passed over me!" he breathed. "God what a laugh for the rats that would be! Damn this radio!"

For savage emphasis, he cracked his free fist against the panel, yelped with pain, and then turned his attention forward. The east sky was fast becoming aglow with the new sun. Shafts of pale yellow light were trying to cut their way through the covering of fog. The overcast clouds had been blown away and the sky above was slowly changing from a dirty grey to the hue of blue steel.

He stared up at it for a moment, half afraid that he would see the armada high above him and winging away at top speed.

The Dornier had a pretty good flying range but he had used up a lot of gas blasting about over Hamburg. Never in a thousand years would he be able to fly all the way back to Hamburg and catch the Bremen there in case he didn't find it off Iceland.

"Nope, just one chance you've got, guy!" he told himself grimly. "If you don't see it in the next ten minutes or so, you're out of luck. It'll be just a tie score between you and that louse, Wolfgang. You blasted some of his radio planes, but he got the Bremen. And what's more, he'll go on living to think up new hell for the Nazis to sling about. His hide is what you really want. His…."

Combat's teeth clicked shut and he sat up stiff in the seat, as though he had been shot. For a full second he stared blankly ahead and down. Then he cursed and drew one hand across his eyes. But it was no dawn mirage of the North Sea. There it was! The Bremen, like a hulky grey-painted ghost, half buried in the rolling fog. He could see clearly the large block letters of her name along each side of the hurricane deck, her rows of life boats, her sturdy superstructure and stacks.

For one crazy instant he could not dispel the belief that he was either dead or dreaming. Many times had he seen that boat at its North River pier in New York, but suddenly to see it looming up out of the fog, hundreds of miles from nowhere, was like a bomb exploding.

And then as the fog seemed to part a bit, cold reality lay before him. The Bremen was under way! But what was a million times more important, twelve large electro-magnetic power cups were clamped to each side, and from the cups large cables ran back to merge in under the giant wings of the magnet planes! THERE WERE six magnet planes in all. Three on each side, with their propellers spinning over. The almost unbelievable was taking place before his eyes. The magnet planes were lifting the Bremen from the water! Lifting her up a foot at a time. The red zinc paint below the water line of the huge ship was visible now. The boat swayed slightly and then grew steady as the magnet planes veered slowly off to each side and took up some of the slack in the cables, until finally the planes were above the Bremen and forming the two top ends of a large V.

The keel was almost clear, now. Combat could see the waters of the North Sea dripping down off the prow. And then, action within him was suddenly released, and he went haywire. In a vicious motion he jammed the nose of his Dornier down at the first magnet plane on the right. Breath clamped in his lungs, he lined up his sights on the hump of glass that covered the pilots' compartment. He remembered that events at Hamburg had proven the cockpit was the only part of the magnet planes that could be affected by his bullets.

"Here I come!" he bellowed as he tore down. "I'll just shoot out your guts, and that should do the trick... I hope!"

He punctuated each word with a savage burst from both guns, but to his horror the glass dome of the cockpit seemed to wink up mockingly at him. In the next second he would have to pull out of his mad dive or else slam right into the thing. But in aerial warfare a second is a long time. It can even span a life on occasion. At any rate, before that last second had clicked away into eternity, Combat saw the heavy glass melt inward, as though consumed by terrific heat, and a tongue of flame leaped up as he pulled out of his dive and zoomed off.

No sooner had he gained a bit of altitude than he wheeled and came tearing down back again, heading for another of the magnet planes. The one forward had dipped by the nose, and even as he jabbed the trigger trips, its huge wing began to fall, then crashed like a gigantic whale into the water. The shock broke it in two and its cables whipped and snapped about like angry snakes. Purple flames belched out, and Combat saw the bow of the Bremen rear high, then fall back into the water.

Then he tore his eyes from the sight and concentrated on the magnet plane beneath him. Once again he poured nickel-jacketed bullets down at the glass dome of the cockpit. And once again it wasn't until the very last second that the glass gave way before the fury of his burst and changed into a column of red flame as though by magic.

"Next!" Combat bellowed and zoomed for more altitude.

However as he leveled off the top of the zoom he did not have the chance to hurl his craft into another dive. True, the Bremen was back in the water and rolling from side to side. But it wasn't that which stopped him. Instead, it was the yammering, blasting death that poured down from above. In a flash he kicked the rudder and belted the Dornier through a whirlwind roll. Then he zoomed up off to the right. And then, and then only, he twisted his head and glanced around. He spotted it almost immediately. A seaplane, with the Nazi insignia on its wings, was tearing down at him with all the fury of a metal vulture. Sight of it, however, brought wild laughter to his lips—wild laughter of pure fighting joy. Why? Because the craft was the same seaplane in which Doctor Wolfgang had fled the Hamburg basin. Even now Bill Combat could actually see that ugly face pressed against the glass of the pilot's compartment.

With a wild whoop he ignored the purple fury below. That job was done. A flash glance had shown him all the magnet planes plunging about in the water, two of them in flames. And in their midst was the Bremen, dancing about like a toy boat, smoke belching from her stacks while her master sought desperately to steam her clear of that purple hell, before it was too late. Whether that could be done, Combat didn't know.

No sooner had he banked than Combat faked a zooming climb. In a flash the Nazi pilot tried to cut him off with blazing guns. But Combat had simply faked the zooming climb. Now he dropped his nose like a rock, purposely lost a couple of hundred feet, then hauled up the nose and practically hung his ship on its prop. Jabbing both trigger trips forward he held them there.

The Nazi tried, yes, but he might just as well have tried to dive his plane to safety down the stack of the Bremen. In short, he didn't stand a chance. For a second or so the seaplane kept on flying through the air. Then suddenly it came apart. The wings came off, as though slashed clear by a knife. The rest of the craft sailed through the air like a sore thumb and then exploded in a roar of sound that shook the very heavens.

Gleefully, he twisted in the seat and stared down into the fog. There was still a faint purple glow far in the distance, but the fog concealed about everything else. And then the Dornier's engine began to sound like a spilled keg of nails on a tin roof.

Eyes straining anxiously, he finally spotted the surface of the water, eased off and made a splash landing. The craft promptly started sinking by the nose. It went half under before it stopped.

"One of these days I'm going to land a plane on solid earth!" he grunted. "It should be a novelty. I...."

He cut off the rest and stared straight ahead. The fog ceiling was a hundred feet or so. Something was churning the waves toward him. It took one glance to tell it was a destroyer. And it took another glance to tell that the flag flying at the masthead was the Union Jack.

TWENTY MINUTES later he was hauled, drenched and dripping, up onto the deck of HMS Spitfire. There a group of wide-eyed officers surrounded him. He didn't give them a chance to ask questions.

"Skip the uniform, I'm no Nazi tramp," he said. "Get moving! Flash word to the other ships around. If the Bremen is still afloat she should be a couple of hundred miles off Iceland. Probably heading for Russia, if her engines are still working after that crack she got."

"The Bremen?" the senior officer of the group exclaimed. "What the devil are you talking about? The Bremen way up here?"

"And damn near flown over you guys and back to Germany," Combat said as weariness started to close down on him.

"The man's crazy, sir," he heard somebody say. "The Bremen's in South Atlantic waters, if you ask me."

Combat started to speak, but he was too damned tired. After all, it must have sounded crazy. And if the Bremen was still steaming, she was a cinch to lose herself in the damn fog. To hell with her, anyway. Wolfgang, and his magnet planes, and his Blau Wave, and the radio torpedoes—they were no more. Let Hitler have the Bremen if he could sneak her down from Russia someday. Repairs would cost him plenty, anyway.

"Yes, take him to the sick bay," somebody said. "We'll turn him over to Intelligence when we make port."

"That's a swell idea," Combat murmured sleepily. "And don't hurry, sir. Take a week, if you like. I'm sure not to... wake... up... before then."

And the last was punctuated by a blissful snore.